Appleton

MAKING THE CUT

The Game Time series:

Off the Crossbar
Rebel Power Play
Making the Cut

MAKING THE CUT

DAVID SKUY

Scholastic Canada Ltd.
Toronto New York London Auckland Sydney
Mexico City New Delhi Hong Kong Buenos Aires

Scholastic Canada Ltd.
604 King Street West, Toronto, Ontario M5V 1E1, Canada
Scholastic Inc.
557 Broadway, New York, NY 10012, USA
Scholastic Australia Pty Limited
PO Box 579, Gosford, NSW 2250, Australia
Scholastic New Zealand Limited
Private Bag 94407, Botany, Manukau 2163, New Zealand
Scholastic Children's Books
Euston House, 24 Eversholt Street, London NW1 1DB, UK

Library and Archives Canada Cataloguing in Publication
Skuy, David, 1963-
Making the cut / David Skuy.
(Game time)
ISBN 978-1-4431-0483-8
I. Title. II. Series: Game time (Toronto, Ont.)
PS8637.K88M34 2010 jC813'.6 C2010-901937-7

Front cover image © Masterfile
Back cover image © iStockphoto.com/Dave Skinner

6 5 4 3 2 1 Printed in Canada 116 10 11 12 13 14

CONTENTS

To the home team
for letting me read at the beach on occasion.

1

THE LETTER

Charlie Joyce held the letter up. "But Mom, an NHL coach will be there. Only eighty players are invited. It's a chance in a lifetime."

"I'm sure it is," she answered softly.

He couldn't understand. Two weeks at the Youth Elite Hockey School — a dream come true — and the perfect way to start the summer. And that after the perfect finish to the hockey season. His team, the Rebels, had won the league championship. And now this!

"Pudge told me all about it. Some of the guys have been talking about it, but I never believed I'd actually get invited. They have a real coaching staff — like I said, we're talking guys who've coached in the NHL — and we're on the ice four hours a day, and there's dry land training and fitness testing . . ."

"It does sound fun."

"And the camp's only two weeks. I'll be back before you know it, and I'll help out at the café every day, I promise. You won't even have to pay me."

His sister Danielle came into the kitchen. "What are you two arguing about?" she said.

"We're not arguing," his mom said.

As if he needed to deal with his irritating kid sister now. "Don't you have somewhere to go?" he snapped.

"I can go wherever I want. It's my house too." She stuck her tongue out.

"You're so lame," he said.

"Stop picking on your sister," his mom ordered.

He couldn't hold his anger in. "This is totally unfair. Danielle gets to go to drama camp, and you won't let me go to the best hockey camp in the wor— "

He stopped — his mom looked like she was about to cry.

"Real nice, Charlie," Danielle said.

"I didn't mean to . . . You don't have to cry, Mom."

His mother sighed and wiped her tears away with her fingers.

"Charlie, I'd like nothing better than for you to go, believe me."

"Then what's the problem?"

She put her hand on his. "I've tried to keep things normal this year, as much as possible. I know you two have been through a lot. After Dad died it was so difficult, what with moving to Terrence Falls, new schools, new friends. I'm so proud of both of you — and Dad would be too. But opening the café was very expensive. Money's really tight right now. If we had two incomes coming in, it would be different . . ."

Her eyes clouded. Charlie felt himself tear up now.

He missed his dad so much sometimes his chest hurt. He couldn't believe it had been a whole year since the car accident. So much had happened since then. He'd gotten through grade nine at his new school and survived the bullying of Jake and his crew. Actually, if it hadn't been for Jake, he probably never would have had the courage to try out for the school hockey team, where he'd met his friends. It was only then that he had started to feel like Terrence Falls could really be his home. It was still so hard to think about his dad, though.

His mom squeezed his hand. "I'm really sorry, Charlie. I want the world for you. Only I'm really stretched financially right now."

He looked at the bottom of the letter. Total cost: $1,450.

"Danielle's got her drama camp in August," she continued. "I've had to replace the vents and the hood for the range at the café, plus replace the grill because I was too stupid to get the extended warranty." She banged her head with her hand.

"That's not your fault," Charlie said. "How were you supposed to know it was going to break down so soon?"

She leaned back in her chair. "Thanks, Charlie. It was a bad decision, however, and one that cost me dearly. I simply can't ask Grandma and Grandpa for more money, either. They've been incredibly generous already. Hockey camp is a bit of a luxury. I'm . . . I'm . . . sorry, Charlie."

She seemed ready to cry again.

"Forget it, Mom. It's cool. Of course I wanted to go. There are more important things."

"What about next year?" Danielle asked.

Charlie took a deep breath. His sister was really bugging him lately. He didn't feel like talking about it with a ten-year-old. But his mom was looking at him with that "be polite" expression.

"The camp is only for fourteen- or fifteen-year-olds. I'll be too old next summer." He pushed his chair back. "I'm gonna watch TV for a bit." His mom looked really upset. "It's okay," he said. "I know you'd send me if you could. There are worse things than hanging out here this summer."

If his mom could have read his mind she'd have known that wasn't even close to being true. He looked at the letter lying on the table in front of him. This was going to be a brutal summer.

"I don't have to go to drama camp," Danielle said suddenly.

Their mother sat up in her chair and looked at her in surprise. "You've been dying to go to that camp for months. I had to beg to get you in. It's all arranged. And Hannah's going with you. I was on the phone for an hour to get you into her cabin."

"I know, Mom, and camp would be good . . ." She squeezed her eyes tight and nodded at Charlie. "But I can go next year. Charlie can only go now."

He couldn't believe his ears. His irritating little sister, who'd been driving him insane about that stupid drama camp for so long that he thought his head would explode, was actually doing this for him?

He was incredibly tempted to let her go through with it too . . . but obviously he couldn't. It wouldn't be right.

"That's totally awesome of you, Danny. But you're too good an actor to miss the camp. You have to go. Besides, Hannah would miss you."

She shook her head. "Mom can use the money from my camp to pay for your hockey. I'll go next summer. I want you to go."

They both looked at their mom. She had tears in her eyes.

"Why are you crying so much today?" Danielle asked.

"You're such wonderful kids," she said. "That's an extremely generous offer, Danielle. Are you sure about this?"

"Totally."

"Really?"

"Really, Mom."

His mom raised both hands into the air. "What do you have to say about that, Charlie?"

He didn't know what to say. "Why don't you think about it for a day or two, Danny. I have until the weekend to accept the offer."

"Don't wait, dude. Live for the moment!"

Charlie laughed and put his arm across Danielle's shoulders. "I think I might have the most totally awesome kid sister — like, in the entire universe."

"What do you think about that?" his mom asked Danielle.

A mischievous look crossed her face. "I think the most totally awesome kid sister in the universe might like some ice cream." She pointed to the fridge.

"No chance," Charlie declared. "The most totally awesome kid sister in the universe does not deserve store bought ice cream. She deserves a banana split with chocolate sauce and sprinkles from Dutch Dreams — on me."

"What about whipped cream?" Danielle exclaimed.

"That's automatic, Danny."

His mom pushed her chair from the table and stood up. "That's simply too tempting. I might have to join in."

Charlie pointed his finger at her. "Don't think of bringing your purse. I've been saving up for this."

In truth he'd been saving for a new long board by doing deliveries for his mom at the café. This occasion definitely called for dipping into his savings, however.

"Let me grab some ice cream money — and then let's do this thing," he said, punching his fist in the air.

He charged out the kitchen, his fist still held up. He felt like flying up the stairs.

The YEHS was legendary. He had to call Pudge.

Charlie slowed down suddenly. How was he going to tell him? Pudge was a solid player, and Charlie loved having him as his left winger, but he probably hadn't received an invite. It might be a bit awkward.

A worrisome thought crept into his mind. He took

his money from the shelf and went back downstairs. He went back to the kitchen and looked at the letter, and his heart sank. The camp started on the same weekend he was supposed to go to Pudge's cottage. Now it was going to be even harder to tell him. Charlie forced that out of his mind. Danielle deserved her banana split, and a few other presents besides that.

They were already outside waiting, and so, with no one around to see, Charlie couldn't help himself — he raised both arms over his head and did a quick victory dance.

The camp started in three weeks — and he'd thought his summer was going to be boring!

DOWNHILL

Charlie slowed down as soon as he heard the familiar voices. He'd been worried about how to tell his friends about the hockey camp. It might sound like he was bragging. He decided he was going to wait until after they'd finished their ride and everyone was about to leave. Then they wouldn't feel weird about it and it would just be over. He rode slowly the rest of the way and casually waved hello.

"Rolls Joyce is in the house," shouted a broad-shouldered, sandy-haired boy. He held out his fist.

"Hey, Scott," Charlie said, giving it a punch and then picking up his long board. "And how is everyone?"

"School's over. What could be better?" a round-faced, chubby boy answered. He nodded towards The Hill. "A few guys are ahead of us. We're just chillin' till it's our turn to ride. You can go down with us."

Charlie sat down next to him. Pudge was his best friend, and the first kid he'd met when he moved to Terrence Falls. Even though they'd only known each other for grade nine, it seemed like they'd been friends forever.

Nick came over. Dark-haired and athletic looking, he was an incredible defenceman, who teamed up with his best friend Scott to anchor the Rebels' defence core. He turned around and patted his own shoulder.

"I just wanted you dudes to get a good look at my back," Nick said. "You'll be seeing it a lot on the ride down."

"I've oiled my wheels," Charlie replied. "Today's all about my spectacular victory."

"You'd better put rockets on that board or you'll be lucky to finish by tomorrow," Nick replied.

Charlie blushed slightly. His board was pathetic and he knew it. Zachary had lent him his brother's old one. The nose was all chipped, and the sides had begun to split. The rollers were chipped and pitted, and no amount of oiling seemed to speed the board up.

"In about a month I'll have the cash for the new board, and then . . ."

A chorus of laughs drowned him out. He'd been talking about a new board forever.

He forced himself to join in. "I'm focused on technique at this point," he said. "Trust me, when the new wheels arrive you'll be lining up for autographs."

"We'll be lining up to race you 'cause of the guaranteed win," Scott said. He gave Charlie a good-natured shove, and held up his board. Charlie looked at it with admiration — it was a truly sweet machine. "Black Beauty and I have decided today is the day to dethrone Sir Zachary of Slowville and become what I have always been destined to be — King of The Hill."

"Maybe King of Marshmallow Cookies," Nick quipped.

Charlie had to laugh at that. Scott's appetite was legendary.

Scott's lower lip began to tremble. "I had that one box of cookies and you humiliate me in front of my peer group."

"You had the box for breakfast, dude."

Scott winked. "Guess what I got in my knapsack right now?"

"What are you waiting for?" Nick exclaimed.

Scott ripped open his knapsack and pulled out a box of raspberry jam marshmallow cookies. Nick reached his hand out, only to have Scott slap it away. Zachary had come riding over The Hill and he slowed to a smooth stop.

"Zachary needs to fill up on junk first," Scott declared, holding the box out to him.

With his usual lopsided grin in place, Zachary ambled over and helped himself to three cookies. He was also the best boarder among them, and had taught Charlie to ride.

"I was gonna let someone else win today," Zachary said. "Unfortunately for you, marshmallows make me stronger. So I'm gonna have to kick your butts . . . again."

"Why didn't I bring chocolate chip?" Scott moaned.

While the guys polished off the cookies, Charlie and

Pudge moved over to the grass under a tree and began putting on their pads.

"I figure we got about five more minutes until it's our turn," Pudge said.

"Scott could eat three boxes in that time," Charlie said.

"Ain't that the truth." Pudge spun the wheels of his board. "My hyper dad's decided we have to leave for the cottage around seven o'clock. I'll try to delay him, but count on an early morning. Once we're there he usually lets people sleep in — until he starts with the power tools, of course."

Charlie knew he had to tell him. He'd been stoked about going to Pudge's family cottage. It was the one thing he was looking forward to all summer. Pudge was going to teach him how to water ski, and there was a bunkie by the water just for them . . . Pudge was going to be bummed out.

"Yeah, about that. Um . . . a little problem."

Pudge looked over.

Charlie picked at the grass. "You wouldn't believe what came in the mail. Well, anyway, I can't believe it. It's sort of unbelievable . . ."

Pudge raised his eyebrows.

"Right. I guess I made that clear. Anyway, I got invited to the YEHS; and, it's a total drag but it starts that weekend . . . so I guess I can't go to your cottage."

He waited for Pudge to get mad or upset.

"That *is* unbelievable. It's totally amazing!" He stood up. "Hey guys. Guess what?"

"Pudge, don't —" Charlie began.

"Charlie's going to the YEHS . . . for real. He got an invitation."

A cheer went up. Scott came over and put his hand on Charlie's shoulder. "It's actually not that prestigious or that big a deal . . ." he said.

Pudge cut him off. "What are you talking about? The best players from the Eastern region at a two-week camp, invitation only, with professional coaches . . . ?"

"Yeah, but I just heard that they're so desperate for players they'll invite just about anyone — for instance, even Nick got invited."

"It gets worse than that," Nick said. "They actually invited . . ." He took a deep breath and dabbed his eye as if to wipe away a tear. "I mean, standards are so low they're letting Scott come." He pretended to break down and cry.

Scott went over and patted him on the back. "It's okay, Nicholas. It's okay. I know it's embarrassing. But if it makes you feel better, there's a four-year-old kid on my street who didn't get an invitation." He screwed up his face and chewed his lower lip. "Actually, that's not entirely true. He got an invitation, but turned it down when he heard that I'm going."

The news was music to Charlie's ears. He'd been excited to go, but at the same time he'd felt a little nervous about not knowing anyone.

"You guys deserve to go; and it looks good on Terrence Falls High to have three players going to the YEHS," Pudge said.

Charlie knew Pudge was a cool guy, but he was super impressed by how little the news about his three friends going to the camp seemed to bother him. It was just the opposite in fact — he sounded really happy. But when he looked over at Zachary, he second-guessed his decision to tell Pudge. Zachary was the most laid-back guy he knew, but he looked kind of upset now. He was an awesome player, and the second leading scorer on the Rebels, playing right wing with him and Pudge. He definitely deserved an invitation.

"I can't believe my bad luck," Zachary said. "I have to go to my Great Aunt Hetty's eightieth birthday party, and I can't go."

"You got an invitation too?" Scott said. "The YEHS is dead to me."

"Couldn't they change the date?" Charlie asked Zachary.

He rolled his eyes. "Don't even ask. I begged. I pleaded. I tried every argument I could think of. Think of it. Pudge gets to go to his cottage and water ski and stuff; you three are going to an awesome hockey camp; and I'm spending four days with a bunch of senior citizens."

They all exploded with laughter.

"Maybe you can organize a wheelchair street hockey game," Scott sputtered.

"I don't suppose you could laugh at someone else?" Zachary said good-naturedly.

"We'll laugh at you for another ten minutes, and then we can get back to laughing at Scott," Nick said.

Pudge pointed to The Hill. "I think we're up soon," he said.

Scott nudged Zachary. "I'll take a rain check and mock you later."

"You're a good guy," Zachary said. "Thanks."

The three of them continued to joke around as they began to strap on their pads.

"So that will be cool — you, Scott and Nick at the camp," Pudge said to Charlie. "I'll talk to my dad about another week for you to come up to the cottage."

"Yeah. That'll be cool. I'll check it out with my mom. For sure, though."

They finished with their pads. Charlie still felt a bit bad about it, and he wondered if he should say something about Pudge not going, just to clear the air.

That's when he heard the voice that always ruined his day.

"So I did this wicked toe grab on the half-pipe, and then get the stupid idea to add a 180. Total epic fail follows, and I take a slide down the wall like a juicy tomato thrown against a window."

Jake Wilkenson. Of course he'd have to show up!

A group of riders appeared over the crest of The Hill. They were all laughing at Jake's story. Charlie instantly picked out the unmistakable long, black hair and Oakland Raiders jersey. Charlie still didn't understand why Jake had it in for him. But it had started the first time they'd met, at a shinny game before grade nine even started. After the game Jake had come up from behind and slew-footed him. Then he'd tried to keep him off the school hockey team. Last season, Jake had given him a concussion with a cross-check from behind.

Charlie didn't have much time for the rest of his crew either — Liam, Thomas and Roscoe. The whole group of them went to Terrence Falls High School, and played for the Wildcats, the team the Rebels had beaten in the finals.

Charlie steeled himself as they rode closer.

Pudge wasn't saying anything either, and Charlie knew why. Jake had bullied Pudge for years.

"The Hill's a bit steep for you, Joyce," Jake sneered. "And Pudge is only gonna break his board with all that weight. I think we should go first."

Charlie noticed Pudge turn pink. He was sensitive about his size. Charlie fought to control his temper.

"Forget him, guys. Let's go," Charlie said.

But Jake wouldn't let up. "Why not let us go first. We'll be down and up before you get ten metres."

"Let's just ride," Charlie said to his friends.

"Step aside, girls. You're embarrassing yourselves," Liam taunted.

"Yeah. I'm in a bit of a hurry. I need to get prepared for the YEHS hockey camp," Jake bragged. "That's right. I was invited. You probably don't know much about it on account of it being for *real* hockey players."

Charlie's heart sank. He probably shouldn't have been surprised. As much as he disliked Jake, he had to admit he was a fantastic player, and it made sense that he'd be invited too. Jake stared at Charlie, and suddenly his jaw slackened and his shoulders slumped. "Don't tell me. Shoot me now. You're going, aren't you?"

"And Scott and Nick too," Pudge shot back. "Zachary also got an invite, but he can't go."

Jake straightened up and smirked. "This'll be a chance for us to get to really know each other," he said.

"You'll find out how really lame they are," Liam said.

"That I already know," Jake said. He pushed off on his board. "You dudes aren't ready. Thanks for letting us go ahead."

His friends laughed and followed him down The Hill before Charlie could say a word.

"Zachary, can I come on that trip with you?" Scott said.

That broke the tension and the boys began to joke about it. Nick made up a story about starting a book club with Jake, and Scott cracked everybody up as he dreamed up creative games he and Jake were going to play together on the bus ride to the camp. Charlie pretended it was all a big laugh — but for him it wasn't. Jake had made grade nine tough for him — very tough — and that cross-check had almost ended his hockey season. Just once he'd like to do something without Jake being around.

Why did he have to exist?

"All clear," the spotter yelled. "Next group can go."

Zachary pushed off, and the rest of them followed. Charlie was preoccupied and was the last to go. At least Jake wouldn't have any of his friends at camp, he reasoned. With Scott and Nick there — and those two could trash talk with the best of them — Jake wouldn't dare go into his bully routine.

He turned the first corner and lowered himself closer to the ground to pick up speed. Zachary was way out in front, and the others were pulling away. His board was really pathetic. He had to get a new one already. A few more deliveries for his mom, and it was his.

Charlie leaned into the second corner, trying to coax a little more speed out of his board.

ROOMMATES

The bus drove through a stone gate and under a wrought iron archway with a banner that read *Northern University*. It followed a tree-lined circular drive bordered by ivy-covered buildings and stopped in front of a squat, two-storey building. The door opened, and a blond-haired woman wearing a blue sweatsuit, the letters *YEHS* written across the chest, leaned up the stairs and waved a clipboard in the air.

"Grab your things and come meet me in front of this building," she said cheerfully. "And welcome to the Youth Elite Hockey School."

The boys on Charlie's bus let out a big cheer and began to file out. Charlie was relieved to finally get off. He'd been late getting to the bus. He and Pudge had been playing some shinny at the rink the day before and he'd forgotten his sticks in Pudge's garage. They had to turn back and get them, and Charlie was lucky to even make it. Unfortunately, the only seat left was in the first row next to one of the coaches. His name was Trevor, a former Northern University player. He was a cool guy, but it was hard to sit with a coach for five hours. It was also painful to hear Jake behind him, talking to a bunch of the guys, pretending to be so nice. It seemed like at least half the players on the bus were Jake's friends by the time they arrived.

"Listen up, boys. Can I have your attention please?" The blond woman held up her clipboard. Most of the boys kept talking. She didn't seem too bothered by it. Slowly, she raised two fingers to her mouth.

Tweet! Tweet! Tweet!

It was the loudest whistle Charlie ever heard, and it worked. They all stopped. She smiled as if nothing had happened.

"Hi. My name's Jen."

"Hi Jen," came some calls from the back.

"I know you're all eager to get going, and excited about the next two weeks. We're looking forward to working with you. I've been told you're a very talented bunch, and the coaches have a fantastic program planned. All I need is a moment of your time so we can organize things. I'm the program manager, which means I'm responsible for making sure everyone gets to where they're supposed to be. Of course, what that really means is that I give the orders and you obey."

A loud chorus of protest was heard from the back. Charlie turned — Jake was in the thick of it, laughing and joking with the guys next to him. Charlie wondered if Jake knew them from before.

Jen cast a gaze their way. "I'm guessing you boys are going to be a problem."

Charlie heard Jake's voice above the others. "We're as good as gold, Jen. I promise."

Jen laughed and rolled her eyes. "I'm sure about that." She pointed her clipboard at two large tables. "Over there you'll see a list with room numbers. When I'm finished talking, I want you to go over in as orderly manner as possible, which probably means like a herd of elephants. Roommates are pre-arranged — no changes, don't even try. Collect your luggage and put it in your rooms, and come back here. Please don't unpack. You'll have time for that later. You'll then return to your bus to grab your hockey equipment and carry it across the field to the rinks. From there, I want you to all go to Rink 1 to meet the coaches."

"Are we playing today?" Jake asked.

Jen shook her head. "I like your enthusiasm, but no, not today. Trust me, you'll have plenty of time on the ice. After the coaches introduce themselves, I'm going to walk you through the program, provide an orientation of the campus, and then you can unpack and have dinner. You'll be on the ice tomorrow." She held her clipboard up again. "Ten minutes, gentlemen, and then I want you right back here."

As predicted, most of the guys stampeded to the tables. Charlie hung back. It was a bit nerve-wracking having a roommate assigned to you. What if he got Jake?

"I don't have to ask your name," Trevor said, when

Charlie got to the front. "Charlie Joyce." He ran his finger down the list. "You're in room 20A — with Corey Sanderson."

Nick and Scott were waiting for him by the bus. "So what rooms are you in?" he asked. "I'm in 20A."

"I'm in 21A," Scott said.

"What about you?" he asked Nick.

"22A. We're all next to each other at least."

"It's like we're a forward line," Scott said, "and I'm the superstar and you two are my useless linemates."

"Hey, Charlie. We should probably tell Scott that he can't talk to us again until camp is over — and be gentle. He's very sensitive," Nick said.

"How about we dump our stuff in our rooms and then we talk about not talking to Scott," Charlie said.

"Come to my room and we'll talk about it," Scott said.

"Sounds good," Charlie and Nick chorused, and all three friends hauled their bags up the stairs to their rooms.

"I'll be over in a sec," Charlie said to Scott, as he pushed open the door to his room.

"You must be the one and only Charlie Joyce."

His roommate came over and held out his hand.

"And you must be Corey," he replied tentatively, giving it a shake.

"Guilty as charged."

Charlie felt totally intimidated. He was supposed to compete against this kid? He was downright huge. Was he really only fifteen?

"I'm from Brunswick. Where're you from?" Corey asked.

His friendly tone put Charlie more at ease.

"I'm from Terrence Falls. It's small. You wouldn't have heard of it."

"Sorry, but I haven't. What league did you play in last season?"

"The East Metro — the EMHL."

He nodded vigorously. "I know that league. Played in a tourney a few years ago against a team from there. You ever heard of a place called . . . now let me think . . . what was the name . . . I remember green sweaters . . ."

"It doesn't matter," Charlie said.

"The rink was red brick — an 'old-school rink,' my dad called it. Nice place too. I can picture the team in my head." He looked out the window and then snapped his fingers. "Got it. Is there a Cliffcrest near you?"

"That's like half an hour from Terrence Falls."

"So I sort of know your hometown. Probably played there." He sighed. "Been in so many rinks I can hardly remember them. Anyway, I took this bed, so why don't you set up over there."

Charlie put his bag on the far bed.

"You weren't here last year, were you?" Corey asked. "I mean, I don't remember you."

"Nah. This is my first year."

Corey nodded a few times. "This is my second. Got invited last year too." He flopped on his bed. "I'm sounding like a jerk, I know." He waved off Charlie's protest. "If you have any questions, just ask.

I know everything that goes on. It can get pretty intense, believe me. Some guys totally crack under the pressure. I love it, though. We have two-a-day practices, along with fitness training. Fitness is my thing, so I'm ready. They take the conditioning part as seriously as the hockey, believe me. You get in shape or they'll kill ya."

"You look like the fitness part won't be a problem."

Corey grinned and patted his stomach. "My dad's a workout maniac. He's got me going to the gym like four times a week, and we got this personal trainer to work on strength and flexibility. I do all sorts of hockey-focused training. This year we worked on quick starts. Built up my legs. Scouts look for that."

"For what?" Charlie asked, bewildered by the non-stop talk.

"Acceleration. Forwards who can drive past a defenceman."

"Have you met a scout?"

"A few," Corey replied nonchalantly. "My dad deals with them, mostly. There'll be scouts at the Challenge Game, and some at a few practices."

"The . . . what game?" Charlie asked.

"Forgot. You're a first-timer. At the end of camp they pick the top twenty players, plus goalies, and we scrimmage. It's not a real championship . . . but it's cool." He laughed. "I'm gonna head down to the bus. Once I get talking hockey . . . feel free to tell me to shut it. I won't mind."

Ring, ring, ring.

Corey reached into his pocket and pulled out a cell phone. "Hi, Dad. We just arrived. Hold on." He put his hand over the receiver. "Good to meet ya, Charlie. I just gotta talk to my dad for a sec." He opened the door, then stopped. "Forgot to ask. What position do you play?"

"I'm usually centre. Not sure where I'll play here, though."

"I'm centre too. Hope we get on the same team."

With that, he left. Charlie tossed his bag on his bed, and went to check out his friends' rooms. They beat him to it, however. The door flew open and the pair of them walked in.

"Could your roommate be any bigger?" Scott exclaimed. "He's like a small mountain."

"His name's Corey," Charlie said. "I think he's a fairly serious player. He was invited here last year, and he's been scouted and has a personal trainer. Anyway, he said that they work us pretty hard."

"As long as they feed us, I say bring it on," Scott said.

"We should get going," Nick said. "Jen told us to hustle."

"Don't be such a worrywart," Scott said, folding his arms across his chest. "We're superstars now, dude. We can do what we want."

They looked at each other.

"I kind of want to go," Charlie offered.

"Me too," Nick said.

Scott thumbed towards the door. "I think it's clear

that we can't be told what to do — so let's hurry before Jen yells at us for being late."

Charlie was the last one out. He hesitated briefly before closing the door.

Hard to believe it was all about to start.

TEACHER'S PET

Charlie waited as the crowd of players walked through the arena doors. He'd overheard someone say there were four rinks, and this one had five thousand seats and was used by the university hockey team. At the top of the stairs he stopped to look for Nick and Scott. He also spotted Jake talking to a bunch of guys.

"Why is it that every kid always wants to sit in the back row?" Jen asked him. "Never could understand that. Follow me — we need to fill up the front."

Charlie felt incredibly dorky following Jen. To complete the humiliation she lowered his chair and pointed to it. He heard some guys laughing.

Jen continued to corral the stragglers, directing them to the front row.

"Quiet down now, gentlemen," she said loudly. "Here comes Coach Clark to introduce the staff."

A buzz of excitement rose as the camp's founder and head coach came through the dressing room tunnel and up the stairs into the stands to face them. Charlie had read the camp website and knew all about him. He was a former NHL player, a rugged defenceman famous for big hits. He'd been coach of the university hockey team for the past twelve seasons. Seeing him in person, Charlie was struck by the intensity of his eyes.

Without warning, Coach Clark began speaking. "I'd like to extend a warm welcome to all of you, newcomers and returning players. This is the twenty-first year for the Youth Elite Hockey School — but judging from my grey hair I'm sure you know that."

The players laughed politely.

"A lot of people like to focus on the star players who have been here. We've had forty-two NHLers through our doors, and almost two hundred fifty boys have played at the major junior or university level. Sure, I'm proud of that tradition. It's not the point of this camp, however."

Clark's powerful frame and the serious way he spoke had caught Charlie's attention, and he listened intently.

"You're here because you earned it, because you represent the best fourteen- and fifteen-year-olds in the Eastern region. You're used to being the best players on your team. So what we have here is an all-star team, and that means you'll have a unique opportunity to test yourself against some serious competition. It's not about winning or losing, or making it to the NHL. It's about learning about yourself, learning how to compete and to improve, learning that you have abilities you've never had to use before because you could get by without them. Well, not here. Here you need to get better, and you do that through hard work."

"As many of you may know, we divide you all into four teams of twenty players each. Some boys take the division of players into teams too seriously, but I urge you not to do that. We try to match up players based on playing styles and complementary skill sets. Throughout the camp we may move players up or down depending on how they're doing. Please, keep things in perspective, and don't worry about where you're placed. We've also been known to make mistakes in judgment, and you'll have lots of time to prove to us what team you should be on."

A smile creased his weathered face. "And believe it or not, you're all going to have fun. This is an elite program, but that doesn't mean it can't be a good time too. So moving on, let me introduce the coaching staff. You've met Jen. She's the program director, and essentially the boss here, so listen to her. Next to Jen is Trevor. He's a former star player on the university team, and we're thrilled to have him here to help coach. He'll be working with everyone at some point. Trevor will also be running the fitness sessions. I understand the early morning runs are particularly fun, right, Trevor?"

The players groaned. Charlie wondered if he was serious.

Four men joined Clark on the stairs. He put his hand on the shoulder of the man next to him. "This is Coach Miller. He's handling Team 1."

Miller barely cracked a smile.

"Coach Miller was assistant coach with me on the Junior National Team, and he also spent eight years in the NHL as an assistant, where he won a Stanley Cup ring with the Dallas Stars."

Miller held up his right hand. There it was — a real, honest-to-goodness Stanley Cup ring. Charlie stared at it in disbelief. He whispered to the guy next to him, "I wouldn't mind having one of those."

Jen shot them a look. "Pay attention, please," she hushed.

Charlie felt himself blush, and he slouched down in his seat.

"Team 2 will be led by Coach Binns," Clark continued. "He's worked at all levels of the game, including the Swiss Elite league." Next he pointed to a tall man with a shaved head. "Coach Williams will handle Team 3. I think he's been coaching at this camp since we opened. Is that right?"

"You and I have been here a long time," he replied.

"And finally, we have Coach Palmer with Team 4. He's a Major Junior A coach, and also coached in Europe for several seasons."

Clark folded his arms. "As I said, this camp is about testing yourself against the best players in your age group. Again, I want to stress that it is not all about making Team 1. Having said that, work hard, compete hard, learn and listen — and if you're lucky, you may get picked to play in the Challenge Game.

"I'm going to turn you over to Jen now as she has some information to go over with you. Things start tomorrow morning, so get a good night's sleep and I know I speak on behalf of the entire coaching staff when I say we look forward to working with you all."

Jen held up her hand. "Please stay seated. I'm going to go over some orientation, hand out the info packages, which have the schedules — very important — and also assign you times for your fitness tests tomorrow."

The coaches waved and walked down the stairs, disappearing into the tunnel leading under the stands. Jen and Trevor began opening some boxes.

While he waited for them to start, Charlie looked around. The arena seemed brand new, with a fancy scoreboard at one end and box seats. The ice glistened under the lights. When he turned to his right he did a double take — J.C. Savard and Burnett were here too!

Not that he should be surprised at that. Savard was probably the best player he'd ever faced, and Burnett was a high-scoring defenceman with a wicked shot. He'd gone up against both of them when he played for his high school team, and also in league play.

That ruled out playing centre for Team 1. Savard would be one centre and Corey would be the other.

Jen stood up, holding a pile of blue folders.

"All I need is your absolute attention for twenty minutes, and then you're free to cut loose before dinner."

A few guys, led by Jake, let out a big cheer. She laughed.

"I need those twenty minutes, though. Coach Clark

is a stickler for time. Don't be late for anything. Please. So I need to go over the schedules."

She walked over to Charlie.

"Would you help me pass these folders around?" She gave Charlie and the guy next to him two large stacks.

Charlie was totally embarrassed. It made him feel like the teacher's pet. When he got near the back row, he heard someone snicker. He didn't need to look to know who it was.

"Thank you very much, Charles. I really appreciate it," Jake said to him as he took a folder.

Charlie gritted his teeth and continued.

"You're very good at this," a kid next to Jake said. "Well done, laddie."

He'd been on their bus, and Charlie had noticed him joking around with Jake.

Charlie didn't answer. Better to ignore them, and who cared if Jake found a few jerks to hang with. Only a jerk would hang with Jake, anyway.

"Let's hurry it up, please. Just hand out the folders, and return to your seats," Jen said.

He hesitated. Was she talking to him?

"You, in the blue sweatshirt. Let's move it."

Charlie handed out the rest of the folders and got back to his seat at fast as he could.

"I really enjoyed that," the other boy said to him as he sat down.

Charlie figured he'd gotten hassled a bit too. "I got a few compliments on my handing out skills," he said.

"Maybe I need to work on mine. I dropped a bunch."

"I'll give you some tips after this," Charlie said.

The boy laughed. "I'm Ben Slogen. Most guys call me Slogger."

"I'm Charlie Joyce . . . I guess most guys call me Charlie."

"Then that's what I'll call you."

Jen interrupted their conversation. "Please turn to page one. This is your schedule, the single most important piece of paper in your life. There's lots of free time to relax and hang out with friends, but we've also put a great deal of effort into maximizing the time you have here. I won't say it again: Be on time! Okay?"

"Yes, Jen. We promise."

Everyone turned. That was Jake, and the guys were all laughing. Charlie rolled his eyes. It wasn't that funny.

Jen seemed to think it was. "Thank you so much, kind sir. I know I can count on you. I hope the rest of you are as dedicated to punctuality. Now, as you can see, wake up is at seven o'clock — and yes, that's in the morning. Everyone better remember to set their alarms."

Charlie forced himself not to groan out loud. Getting up in the morning wasn't exactly his strong suit. Most days he had to sprint to make his first class. No one else reacted, so he kept quiet.

"We have fitness testing to start the day tomorrow, and then your first practice is in the afternoon. Check the bulletin board in the cafeteria for a list of names and which rink you'll be playing in . . ."

Charlie looked at the schedule. It was packed — hockey, hockey, and more hockey.

Could he compete with these guys? Slogger looked like a serious player too. He was taller than Charlie and had thick legs and broad shoulders.

They'd find out soon enough.

5

HOLD THE BUS

Charlie turned over, punched his pillow, and flopped back down. He was tired. Curfew was ten o'clock, but he'd been too stoked to fall asleep for a long time. Jen had warned them about being late, so he tossed the blankets off and forced himself to get up. Wouldn't be such a bad thing to have a relaxing breakfast. Corey had told him all about the fitness testing, and warned him not to eat too much. He'd better tell Scott, not that he'd listen.

"Hey, Corey. Want to grab some breakfast?"

No answer. Corey's bed was empty. Maybe he was in the bathroom?

"Yo, Corey. You ready to go?"

Again, no answer.

That's when he noticed the alarm clock — 8:55. The bus was leaving in five minutes for the fitness centre. How was that possible? His heart pounding in his chest, Charlie whipped on his sweats and sprinted out the room.

A bus was pulling away as he bolted out of the building. He tore down the road waving frantically. The bus stopped and the doors opened. Jen stood at the top of the stairs, hands on her hips, one eyebrow raised.

"So who do we have here?" she asked, as he got onto the bus.

"I slept in . . . I guess," Charlie stuttered.

"I guess you did," she agreed. "First day — probably not the best start. What's your name?"

"Charlie Joyce," he said meekly.

"Mr. Joyce. Could you promise not be late again? Please. Then we can just forget about this little incident."

"I promise. The alarm didn't go off. I had some trouble figuring it out, and . . ."

"Consider it forgotten. Please have a seat. Driver, we can get going."

More than a few guys gave him looks as he walked down the aisle looking for a seat. Scott and Nick weren't on this bus. Who would he sit with? Near the back, a kid waved his hand and pointed next to him. Charlie made a beeline over and sat with a grateful smile. It was Slogger.

"You like to cut it close," he quipped.

"Pathetic, I know," Charlie said. "I was lucky to even wake up."

"Not that lucky. Fitness testing can't be all that fun."

A shadow caught his attention. Jen stood next to him with her hand out. "Mr. Joyce, you forgot to give me your fitness test form."

His heart sank. He'd left it in his room.

"I might've forgotten it . . . I was in a rush to get here and . . ."

She leaned down. "Mr. Joyce, please don't be my problem kid. I always have one." She reached into a folder and pulled out a sheet of paper. "I need you to try a little harder — everyone else got on the bus and brought their form, and I must have told you five times during orientation." She took a deep breath. "Here's an extra. Fill it out, and give it back to me at the Fitness Centre."

"Yes, ma'am."

"Jen is fine. I hate to think I'm old enough to be a ma'am quite yet."

"Sorry about that . . . Jen."

She went back to the front.

"Nice bed head, dude," someone said, a few rows back.

Were they talking about him?

Charlie's stomach growled. He'd slept right through breakfast. He lowered his voice. "Be honest. Is my hair that bad?"

Slogger made a sour face.

"I'm such a loser. Just once I'd like to be on time for something."

As inconspicuously as possible he tried to straighten his hair with his fingers.

* * *

"Group 2, over to the mat area."

He forced himself to his feet. Sweat poured down

his forehead. He'd only just finished the stationary bike test. His legs were still quivering — now what?

He joined his group in front of Jen.

"Can I have your form?" she said to him.

She crinkled her nose and took the paper with two fingers. Some of his sweat had dripped on the page.

"Soggy form-itis — you are having an interesting day, Mr. Joyce."

A tittering of mocking laughter sounded behind him.

"Divide into pairs," she continued. "One guy is a counter — the other will be doing push-ups. I want proper form. The nose and chest must hit the mat or they don't count. I'll be watching, so no cheating. Do as many as you can in two minutes."

They paired up quickly. As Charlie looked around for a partner, another player ran by and knocked Charlie into someone's back.

"What's your problem?" the guy snarled.

He towered over Charlie. It was the kid who was sitting with Jake yesterday at the rink.

Charlie saw Corey skid to a halt near the stationary bikes. Had he run into him? No time to figure that out, unfortunately. He had to deal with a more immediate problem.

"Sorry," he said to him. "I . . . someone banged into me. I didn't mean to . . . sorry."

The guy grimaced. "Just watch where you're going."

"Mr. Joyce, you seem a tad confused," Jen said.

Charlie stared back. What did she want now?

"I told you to get a partner." She pointed at the big player. "Join up with Zane."

Definitely not his first choice.

Zane glared down at him. "You go first. I'm still puffin' from the bike."

Charlie would have liked a rest too, but didn't dare protest, not after bashing into him. Jen was tapping her clipboard impatiently. He dropped to the mat and took a few deep breaths.

"Go!" Jen ordered.

He was caught off guard and was the last to begin. Out of the corner of his eye he saw Jen write something in her notebook. Must be something about him. He picked up the pace. Charlie tried to do a hundred push-ups every morning, so he was pretty good at them. Eventually, his arms began to tremble under the strain. Two minutes must be almost up, he figured.

"Forty-five seconds left!" Jen announced.

Impossible! No way he could keep going.

"Third period, boys," he heard Jen say. "Who's got what it takes?"

Charlie summoned all his energy and pumped out another twenty. Sweat poured into his eyes and dripped onto the mat. He had to stop. His arms and chest were on fire. A few others were on their knees or even flat out on their stomachs. He forced himself up — ten more and that's it, he told himself.

"The final fifteen seconds!"

He willed himself to do four more and then collapsed on the mat as Jen called out, "Time."

"You did 81," Zane said, lips pursed and eyebrows raised. "Not bad for a skinny guy."

He wasn't sure that was a compliment, but said, "Thanks," all the same.

Zane started off strongly. At 45 seconds, to Charlie's surprise, he dropped to a knee and stayed there until the one-minute mark. He struggled to do a few more, then quit.

"How many?" he gasped.

"Forty," Charlie told him.

"Add a few, will ya?" he said. "I suck at these."

Charlie struggled with his conscience while he waited for Jen. Should he lie? Zane had been kind of nasty to him, but then again he had knocked into him. As she stopped before him, Charlie figured it wouldn't hurt anyone to add a few.

"Who was your partner?" Jen asked.

"Zane. He did 65."

Charlie felt himself flush and his chest begin to pound. He prayed she wouldn't notice. Fortunately, she wrote the number without a word and then gave him his form.

"You boys go over to the bench jump," she said, pointing to the far end of the gym.

"What did ya tell her?" Zane asked eagerly when they were out of earshot.

"I added 25," Charlie whispered.

Zane looked disgusted. "Wilkenson was right. You are lame. That's still way less than you. Keep your head up on the ice, doofus."

Zane stomped off, leaving Charlie totally bewildered. A hand patted him on the shoulder.

"Why's Zane mad at you?"

It was Corey. He was breathing heavily and his shirt was soaked in sweat.

"I . . . um, don't exactly know."

Corey whistled softly. "Careful with him. He's a serious defenceman, and dirty as they come. He'll put your head through the boards and laugh about it. I've seen him do it too."

"Thanks," he said wearily. Like that's what he needed — more enemies.

"So how are you doing?" Corey asked.

"Okay, I guess — as long as Zane doesn't kill me first. What about you?"

"I usually do pretty good at the testing." Corey laughed and bounded off to the next station.

Where did he get his energy? Charlie felt all stiff and tired. Tough to jump out of bed and start exercising — and on an empty stomach. He wiped the sweat from his forehead with the bottom of his T-shirt. One more station. Could he just get through it without messing up?

Charlie made sure to be first in line for the next rotation. He'd been late enough today to last a lifetime.

"Joyce, no butting. Get to the back."

Zane pulled Charlie's shoulder and pushed him aside. A few of the guys laughed openly. Charlie whirled around. Zane stared back with a goofy grin and puffed out his chest.

Trevor motioned Zane to come forward before Charlie could react.

"Here's the exercise," Trevor explained. "Start on one side of the bench. When the whistle blows, you hop back and forth over the bench for two minutes." He grinned broadly. "Hockey players need two strong legs and a brain. We'll work on the brain part later. Now we test the motor."

"Zane, you've been through this before. Show 'em how it's done."

As with the push-ups, he started out strongly and tired badly after the initial burst. He ended up with 74.

The instructor pointed at Charlie. "You're next."

"Bet the dude trips before he gets 10," Zane said.

Charlie winced. That guy was becoming a curse. He readied himself, and focused on the exercise. Zane had obviously gone out too fast. He decided to keep a more even pace. The strategy worked. At the one-minute mark, he'd already blown Zane out of the water.

"You're at 80," Trevor encouraged. "Keep going."

Charlie went faster. He'd show Zane. For the final fifteen seconds he went crazy, his feet flying back and forth over the bench.

"Time!"

Trevor put a hand on his shoulder. Charlie struggled to control his laboured breathing. "Congrats, Charlie. You just got the highest total today — 155." He pointed to the next kid in line. "Let's see if you can top that."

No one did. The closest score was 118. A couple of guys looked at him differently, he thought. Not Zane, though. He made it clear he wasn't impressed. Charlie spotted Scott and Nick sitting on a large mat, and joined them.

"How'd the fitness test treat you, dudes?" Charlie asked.

"I think I set a record at each station," Scott said.

"A record for lowest score," Nick said.

"And I bet no one will beat it for the rest of camp," Scott answered proudly.

Slogger came over. "That's enough exercise for one morning. I barely ate breakfast, and now I could eat a horse I'm so starved."

"Please don't mention food," Scott said. "A horse would barely make a dent in my appetite. I need to swim in a sea of French toast, cereal, eggs and chocolate milk."

Charlie rubbed his stomach. "Stop complaining. I slept in and missed breakfast. I'm gonna pass out if I don't eat soon." He suddenly had an odd sensation of being watched.

"Hey, Charlie. How did you do?" Corey asked intensely.

Charlie wondered where he'd come from. "Okay . . . I guess."

"How many push-ups?"

He didn't want to say in front of his friends. "Don't remember exactly."

"Did you do more than 70?"

Corey's eyes were wide apart, his voice very serious.

"Maybe . . . a few more," he said finally.

"What about the bench jump. Did ya beat 152?"

"I'm too tired to remember."

This was a bit weird. He needed to change the subject.

"I should introduce you. Scott, Nick, Slogger, this is my roommate, Corey Sanderson."

Corey immediately brightened up. "Good to meet you guys. How do you know each other?"

"I go to the same school with Scott and Nick, and Slogger and I met at orientation," Charlie said.

"Gotcha. Cool." He cleared his throat. "What positions do you play?"

"We're defence," Scott said, pointing at Nick. "But he's kinda useless."

Corey looked confused, as if he didn't understand.

"I'm a defenceman too," Slogger said.

Corey got up and laughed. "Great to meet you guys. I'll catch up with you later, Charlie."

He moved over to sit with some guys Charlie didn't know. Nick nudged Charlie and looked at him intently.

"What?" Charlie asked.

"What's with all the questions? Bit over the top, don't ya think?" Nick said.

"I don't really know him," Charlie said. "He seems all right, though. A little hyper, maybe. But speaking of over-the-top behaviour, listen to this." He was about to tell them about Zane when Jen called for their attention.

"Sorry for the wait. We had to tabulate the results. This year the player with the best fitness score wins a new Easton stick. Coach Clark wants to show you the importance he places on fitness." A murmur rose among the players. "So, the player with the highest score is — Charlie Joyce."

Nick, Scott and Slogger cheered and punched him good-naturedly. Charlie blushed — but this time it felt good, especially after the way the morning had gone.

"But unfortunately, and here's a lesson for you all, Mr. Joyce was late for the bus this morning and forgot his form. I told you yesterday how vital it is to keep to the schedule. You have to be responsible for yourself, on and off the ice.

"So we deducted 50 points from Mr. Joyce's score. Therefore, the winner of the fitness test is Corey Sanderson."

Charlie's stomach did a flip-flop. He felt sick. The boys around Corey clapped him on the shoulders. Corey's grin seemed too big for his face.

"That's a bit unfair," Slogger muttered.

Charlie prayed he wouldn't tear up. He took a couple of deep breaths. Maybe Slogger was right, but he could only blame himself. Stupid not to set his alarm properly.

"It's eleven o'clock, boys," Jen said. "Why don't we go for a nice, little run — to build up an appetite for lunch."

All the players groaned.

"Not too far," she said. "Just to get the kinks out. After lunch it's a one-hour rest period — then we hit the ice." That drew a cheer. "Now follow me."

She took off towards the door. There was a logjam, so Charlie waited in line. Trevor grasped Charlie's arm.

"Don't worry about it," he said. "You did fantastic on the tests. Jen honestly felt bad about it, only she made such a big deal about being punctual and thought she had to do something to show she was serious. Put it behind you."

Charlie didn't know what to say. "Thanks, Trevor. I guess I can do better with the schedule." He lowered his head. "I kinda have a problem with being places on time. I'm pathetic."

"We think you're pathetic too," Scott said.

"It won't happen again," Nick said. "We'll be his parents. Now be a good little boy and eat your vegetables."

"That sounds like a great idea," Trevor said. He pointed to the door. Everyone else had gone. "You might want to get going now."

"Thanks, Trevor," they chorused, and took off laughing.

Outside the door they all tried a group high-five while running and almost ended up flying into a bush. They were barely able to keep going they were laughing so hard, and Charlie felt grateful his friends were here. He couldn't imagine what this camp would be like if he was alone.

HIGH RISK

Charlie shuffled forward, cradling the puck on his forehand, waiting for his turn. Clark hadn't lied about the hard work — the practice was intense. Drills lasted almost an hour, and they were brutal. Nick and Scott were on another rink, but Corey was with him. Charlie was still struggling to catch his breath, as he waited for the one-on-one drill to start. He felt good so far. At least his skating held up, and he'd been at or near the front almost every time. He was kind of surprised to find he was faster than Corey. It was weird because he looked fast, his form was perfect and he started off great. He just didn't take it into high gear. Maybe he was saving it up since he was here last year and the coaches knew him. The big centre worked hard, though, and never let up, not even for one drill.

At the far end, Corey was ready to go, and Slogger came out to defend. Charlie was interested in seeing what each of them could do. Slogger had already impressed him with his quickness. Corey drove hard to centre, and then about eight feet from the blue line he head-faked left and then cut sharply to the outside. Slogger calmly pivoted on his left foot and forced Corey into the boards. It looked like Corey was cut off, but he refused to give up and continued on to the goal. Slogger lowered his shoulder and knocked Corey off the puck, and pushed it to the back boards with his stick. He then turned to rejoin the defencemen.

Corey still didn't stop. He raced over and pulled the puck back from behind the net, pushed off in front of the crease, and reaching around the goalie shovelled in a backhand on the stick side.

"Guy's a total nut job," someone said.

Charlie didn't have time to think about it. He was next.

He took off hard to gain maximum speed, and then he slowed slightly. The defenceman, a kid named Markus, slowed to match his pace, with one hand on his stick and the other held up shoulder height. He was fairly tall, so Charlie figured he was the poke checker type. As he crossed the red line, Charlie threw in a stutter step and drove outside on his forehand. The defenceman turned slightly, ready to head him off. Charlie faked an inside move. The defenceman overreacted and shifted his shoulders that way. Charlie immediately turned on the jets, continuing on the outside, leaving the defender flat-footed. About fifteen feet from the goal, Charlie cut into the slot. He thought of faking a forehand and going glove side with a backhand deke, when the goalie came out and dropped into a butterfly. The top of the net was totally exposed. Charlie snapped a wrist shot over the goalie's shoulder on the short side.

The defenceman brushed against him as he cut to rejoin the forwards in the corner. "Try that chicken move again and I'll drop you," he growled before skating off.

The fun of scoring melted away. Coach Clark had said camp would be competitive. Probably no surprise that some guys would take it over the top.

Charlie took a couple more turns, fortunately not against Markus. He scored on his last try too. The defenceman kept backing in, so Charlie fired a low shot three feet inside the top of the circle between the defender's legs and right through the goalie's five-hole.

Binns blew his whistle.

"Black shirts down at the far end for shooting practice. Red shirts stay here. Let's move it, boys."

The players wearing black skated off. Binns drifted to the blue line, counting as he went.

"Excellent. We have ten players. I'm going to pair you up. One player stands at the top of the circle. The second player is behind him. I'm going to dump the puck into one corner. The first player to touch the puck is the forward and he tries to score. The second player defends. Play ends when my whistle blows. If the puck turns over, your roles switch."

He picked two players who were standing together. "Why don't you two show 'em how it's done." The two players skated over. "What are your names?"

"I'm Simon."

"Gabriel."

"Sounds good. We'll have Simon in front."

Charlie had noticed these two. Gabriel could absolutely fly, and he was a wizard with the puck. Simon was a powerful skater and had a wicked shot.

Binns fired the puck into the corner. Simon got there first and cut hard to his right, carrying it behind the net, holding Gabriel off with his right arm. As he passed the far post, he spun, reversed directions, and tried to force his way to the front. Gabriel stuck his hips back, forcing Simon to go wide. Simon kept the puck to the hash marks, pulled it towards his skates with the tip of his stick and snapped off a quick shot. It was a cool move, although Gabriel got in the way and the puck deflected off his shin pad and bounced harmlessly to the far corner. Before they could give chase the whistle blew.

"Nice positioning, Gabriel," Binns said. "Notice how he didn't overcommit. Stay in front of your man, using your stick to force him outside. Simon, that was nice puck control, and a nifty try to get the shot off. Good work, both of you."

Binns tapped his stick and nodded at Charlie and Zane. "How about you two give it a go."

Charlie relished the challenge. He'd show Zane a thing or two. The guy was huge, but Charlie was willing to bet he wasn't that fast. He'd use his speed to blow by him. The puck went to the left corner, and Charlie raced after it. As he expected, Zane was slower, which gave him a few feet to work with. Charlie faked with his forehand, lowering his left shoulder and scooping up the puck on his backhand. What he didn't expect was Zane being in the perfect spot, stick extended in his right hand, his left hand held high.

But Zane wouldn't be expecting Charlie's favourite move — puck between the legs and the 360 spin.

The puck part went fine. The 360 spin ran into one problem: Zane's shoulder. Charlie bounced off him and nearly lost his footing. Zane grabbed the loose puck, went in alone and fired a shot into the goalie's stomach.

"Useless shot," Zane cried, and slapped his stick on the ice. "Way to put it right on him."

Binns held his hand up and gave Zane a high-five. "Nice play. No panic. As for the shot, well, why don't you stay a defenceman."

Zane laughed and rejoined the group. Binns looked over at Charlie. "You did well to retrieve the puck, nice speed. You need to be more careful, though. That was a very high-risk play. The point of this drill is to heighten the danger of losing the puck. If the defenceman has you, hold on to the puck and look for an opportunity."

While Binns organized the next two, Charlie fretted over his poor play. Binns was right. He vowed never to underestimate anyone at this camp again, even a musclehead like Zane. Binns couldn't have been too impressed by that effort. Zane had made him look ordinary.

Coach Clark had been right. Everyone at this camp was solid, and he couldn't expect all his usual tricks to work.

After a few other pairs went, Binns said, "Why don't

we try Charlie and Zane again? This time Zane is in front."

Charlie had to strain to see around Zane's broad back. He knew he needed to show Binns something this time. The puck was lofted to the right corner, and Charlie cut inside Zane's left shoulder and flew after it with short choppy strides. His move surprised Zane and they both arrived at the puck at the same time. Zane then surprised him by easing up slightly, allowing Charlie to touch it first.

Then he wished he hadn't. Zane drove Charlie into the boards so hard he lost his wind for a second. Both of them bounced off. Charlie looked down, all the while fighting for breath. The puck remained against the boards. Before Zane could recover his balance, Charlie knifed the puck on his backhand and swooped between him and the post. The goalie threw out his paddle for a poke check, a smart move that would have worked if Charlie hadn't transferred the puck to his forehand a second before. He took two steps across the front of the net and swept the puck into the far side — just before Zane's stick whacked him on the right forearm.

The whistle blew and Binns let out a loud, "Hurrah!"

"Finally, a goal on this drill. Love it. That was hard — that was hockey. You all see that focus by Charlie? He took the hit, kept his cool, and made a play on the net. Zane, don't give up after the hit. These guys don't fall down too easy."

The next pair lined up. Charlie was smarting from

the slash, and still winded from the hit; but Binns's praise took the sting out of it. If that's what it took to score a goal at this camp — then that's what he'd do.

And maybe Zane wouldn't underestimate him, either.

CIRCUS ACT

BEEEP! BEEEP! BEEEP!

Charlie turned the alarm off, relieved that it had worked, and tossed the covers to the side. He'd spent ten minutes checking and rechecking the alarm last night. As he got dressed he felt unfamiliar pains in his legs and shoulders, and then it dawned on him that he was actually sore from the fitness testing and the practice.

"I feel like an old man," he said to Corey, twisting his back and flinging his arms windmill style to loosen up.

Corey didn't answer.

"Wake up, Corey. Breakfast is in thirty minutes."

Charlie shook his head. His roommate was amazing that way — already gone. Did he ever sleep? Charlie finished dressing quickly. He wanted to knock on Scott and Nick's door this time.

Bang. Bang. Bang. Nick and Scott walked in.

"Did you guys sleep outside my door?" Charlie said. "Let me wake you up for once."

"Joyce, your pathetic attempt to wake up early can not defeat my awesome ability to rise at an ungodly hour," Scott said.

"I woke you up this morning," Nick declared.

"What I meant was Charlie's pathetic attempt to wake up early cannot defeat my awesome ability to be woken up by Nick . . ."

"It's too early for me to listen to this," Nick said. "I need breakfast first."

"Is it too early to listen to this?" Scott said. He began to imitate a chicken.

"Where's the roommate?" Nick asked Charlie as they left for the cafeteria.

"Dunno. He's like The Shadow. The guy disappears on me all the time."

"Maybe he has super powers," Scott said excitedly, "that allow him to turn into a white mist and slip under the door . . ." He trailed off. "It's too early for that too, isn't it."

"We'll tell you when to talk again," Nick said.

Scott paid no attention. "Joyce, I'm not sure about your roomie. He kinda scares me."

Scott got along with almost everyone, so his comment took Charlie by surprise. "He's okay," Charlie said slowly. "Like I said before. He's a little intense, is all. Give him a chance."

Nick didn't look convinced. "If he can play, then all's forgiven. If he hangs out with Jake, forget it."

Charlie knew Nick was joking, but it bothered him that his friends had taken a dislike to Corey so quickly.

"There's my roomie," Scott said suddenly, and he ran ahead. "Hey, Sloggermeister. Wait up." He clapped Slogger on the back. "Yo, Slogger. You can't go to breakfast without us. You won't understand the delicate balance between fruit and fibre."

That broke Slogger up. "You're a twisted young man," he said.

Then he and Scott did a hilarious pretend handshake, which started with a patty-cake, and ended with elbow strikes, flapping arms, and two fingers wiggling behind their ears.

Scott, Nick and Slogger cracked jokes and dissed each other all the way to the cafeteria. Charlie followed along, struggling to keep up with the rapid-fire conversation. He'd always envied Scott and Nick for how easily they made new friends and could talk to anyone. Charlie was usually at a loss for words when he was with people he didn't know well.

There was a fairly long lineup for the food. Charlie took a tray and joined it. Still only half-awake, he looked around the cafeteria. Jen was wheeling a large whiteboard against a wall. A bunch of early risers were already finished eating, Corey among them. He was holding court, gesturing wildly, to a table full of listeners.

"Ladies and gentlemen." A loud voice jarred Charlie out of his sleepy thoughts. "For your amusement and pleasure, I shall attempt the impossible. Behold the great Jakerini, who shall attempt to juggle three eggs with a bowl of cereal on his head."

That got everyone's attention.

"Ten bucks says he drops it all."

"A hundred bucks says he falls on his butt."

Jake laughed and bowed to the crowd. "I thank you for your encouragement. I require silence, please; and do not attempt this on your own. I am a professional, and you could get hurt."

"Or end up looking like a doofus," someone quipped.

Jake laughed, and then slowly placed the cereal bowl on this head.

"Ta da!"

The guys clapped loudly, and a chant went up.

"Jug-gle! Jug-gle! Jug-gle!"

Jake raised the three eggs — and he actually began to juggle. Everyone went crazy, whistling and clapping in appreciation. He caught the eggs — and that's when the cereal bowl fell, and the milk splashed all over his shirt and sweatpants.

Charlie would have felt sorry for him — if it hadn't been Jake. Talk about awkward.

Only Jake didn't look the slightest bit upset. He was laughing his head off, and so was everyone else. He bowed deeply.

"Can you juggle bowls of soup next?" someone asked.

"How about spaghetti and meatballs?"

"Thank you. Thank you. I'll be performing here all week." Jake picked up the bowl and put it on his head like a hat, took his food tray back from Zane, and a large group of guys followed them to a table.

Scott leaned over to Charlie. "I always knew he belonged in a circus 'cause he's such a clown."

Charlie was too stunned even to laugh. This wasn't the Jake he knew. Where was the bully who took himself so seriously and picked on people all the time? He'd only met Slogger and Corey, and he barely knew them. Jake was already friends with half the camp.

Charlie never ate a big breakfast, especially this early, and so he helped himself to some cereal and an orange juice and joined his friends.

"So what happens today?" Scott asked.

"Did you forget to read your schedule? Jen will be terribly disappointed," Nick said.

"Of course I read it. I'm just testing you."

Corey had spent half an hour last night explaining the schedule to Charlie, so he practically knew it by heart.

"First, we get divided into our teams," he said. "Then we meet our coaches, when we'll be given a binder with practice drills and forechecking and defensive schemes sketched out. Then we have our first team practice. That's followed by lunch, down time for an hour, during which my roommate will do tons of sit-ups and push-ups or go for a run . . ." That got a laugh from Nick and Scott and a quizzical look from Slogger, "and then a second practice. According to Corey, we definitely will not scrimmage today. No chance. Then it's free time to dinner, and there's a movie in the cafeteria until curfew at ten."

All three guys began clapping.

"Joyce, if you studied this hard in school your marks would be way higher," Scott said.

"Attention over here," Jen announced. "I've posted today's schedule on the bulletin board — and the rosters for the four teams." She gestured to the whiteboard behind her. All the players began talking at once.

"Quiet down, boys. Let Jen finish," Trevor pleaded.

The announcement proved too exciting however, and a low murmur continued. "You've got another five minutes to eat," Jen said, "so finish your breakfast. You'll see the teams soon enough — believe me, you'll need the energy. Once you've seen your team, please go to the conference room with your team number. Team 1 meets in room one, et cetera. Not too difficult, even for hockey players."

Jake's table roared at Jen's joke.

She pointed at the board again. "Following the meeting, which will take about an hour, you'll go to your designated rink for the morning practice."

She'd barely finished before a horde of players charged to see the teams.

"Don't those losers know I'm the only one who made Team 1," Scott said.

Charlie almost choked on his toast laughing. Scott had a way of saying anything and making it funny.

"You think you're a funny guy?" Zane glared at Charlie, his fists clenched. "Let's take a walk outside where the coaches won't interrupt."

Dumbfounded, Charlie stared back. What was he talking about?

"Why don't you call me a loser to my face, loser," he thundered.

So that was it. Zane thought he'd made the joke, and had misunderstood what Scott said.

"Zane, no one was dissin' you. My buds and I were joking around. It's cool."

"What's cool is me putting my fist through your head," Zane growled, taking a step forward.

Charlie's heart was beating wildly. He wasn't afraid of a fight, but he certainly didn't look forward to messing with Zane. He knew firsthand how strong he was. Behind him he noticed Jake smirking. Did he put Zane up to this?

"Like I said, we weren't talking about you."

Zane turned to Jake. "This dude's lamer than a cold grilled cheese sandwich. You actually go to school with this wiener?"

Jake shrugged. "Chill, man. We're all fellow campers." He came over and pulled Zane aside, clapping him on the shoulder a few times. "There's no point fighting him — he's not in your league."

All the guys at his table got up and followed them to the board. Zane turned around, and with his right hand pointed two fingers to his eyes and then back at Charlie.

"Does he need glasses?" Scott joked.

"What's his name?" Slogger asked.

Charlie's heart was still thumping. "It's Zane," he managed.

"More like Insane," Nick said.

Charlie told them about his run-in with Zane at the fitness test.

"At least we know his push-ups are weak," Scott said.

"I don't think too much of him is weak. He's one big dude," Slogger said.

"And ugly," Scott added.

"Let's see where we're playing," Charlie suggested. He didn't need to be reminded about Zane's size.

The guys were still crowding around the lists so Charlie couldn't see them at first. Over the shoulder of one kid he noticed that Nick was on Team 3, and then he saw Scott's name under Team 4. To his surprise Corey was on Team 3. Jake was on Team 2. He felt a bit lightheaded as he looked to the final list.

He couldn't believe it: Charlie Joyce — Team 1.

Slogger elbowed him. "We're teammates. Be nice to me and I'll pass to you once in a while."

Charlie ran down the Team 1 list. Savard and Burnett had made it, as had Simon and Gabriel. His heart sank a bit when he saw Zane had too; Slogger's name was under his.

Scott clapped Charlie and Slogger on the back. "Well done, Joyce. Bloody good show, Sir Sloggster."

Charlie wondered if Scott was miffed at being on Team 4. "You'll move up quick," Charlie said to him, "once the coaches see you play. What can you tell from one practice."

"I agree," Scott said, with his usual good humour. "It takes time to recognize my genius on the ice."

Nick didn't look too happy. "Charlie's right," he said. "You'll be moved up by next practice, I bet."

For all their dissing, they were best friends, and Charlie could tell Nick wanted Scott to be on his team.

For a moment Scott didn't look too happy either. "Doesn't matter," he said. "It'll be fun." A big grin crossed his face. "Besides, think how spectacular my rise to fame will be when I'm selected MVP of the Challenge Game."

"I believe that stands for Most Valuable Princess?" Nick said.

"It does?" Scott said, as if thunderstruck. "Now that's embarrassing."

They kept up the jokes on the way to their respective rooms. Charlie really believed Scott would soon move up from Team 4. He was too good a player, but as a defensive defenceman, the coaches probably didn't appreciate him yet.

Scott stopped before a door with a large number 4 written on a piece of paper. "I'm not sure where Team 4 is meeting. I'll go in here and ask."

"I'm lost too," Nick said, pointing to a door with a 3. "I'll go ask in there."

Charlie waved goodbye and he and Slogger continued on until Slogger spotted the Team 1 sign down another hall. They were about to turn that way when Charlie saw Corey standing by an exit. He figured Corey would be upset by not getting on a higher team.

"I'll catch up with you in a sec," Charlie said to Slogger. "I just wanna speak to my roommate."

Charlie didn't quite know what to say, but thought at the very least he could say hi. As he got closer he saw that Corey was actually on his cell phone. He had a hand cupped to one ear, and his face was pressed into a corner. It was a little noisy in the hall, but it still looked weird being all twisted up like that.

"Hey, Corey," he began.

Corey kept talking.

"Yo, Corey," he said louder.

No response.

Charlie tugged on Corey's sleeve, which startled his roommate so much he practically jumped out of his skin. Charlie started to laugh, but then stopped abruptly. Corey's face was pale, almost ghostly, as if all his blood had been drained away.

"I gotta go. Bye," Corey said, and he closed his phone.

"Are you . . . okay?" Charlie asked tentatively. "Are you sick or something?" At a closer look, he thought Corey had been crying.

"I'm fine," he scowled. "Maybe I am a little sick." He stuffed his phone in his pants pocket. "Can you believe it? Team 3! Isn't that the biggest joke ever? Isn't that totally stupid?"

Charlie wasn't sure if he was asking or telling him.

"I was explaining to my dad how messed up the coaching is this year. He won't listen." Corey hung his head. "He's right, though. I wasn't focused at the practice. I thought I was in for sure because I was here last year. Dad says you gotta be intense every practice, every shift. You can't take a day off, not at this level. But I smoked the skating drills, didn't I? You saw me. And I scored on some one-on-ones. Why'd they put you on Team 1 and me on Team 3. I mean, is that fair?"

Charlie shook his head.

"I'll see ya back at the room," Corey said, and stomped off.

Charlie watched him go, too freaked to even say goodbye. So much for cheering him up. He sure did speak to his dad a lot. He'd talked to him for almost an hour before going to sleep last night. The thought of being able to call his dad any time he wanted made him sad, so he forced it out of his mind and hurried to Team 1's room. He opened the door slowly. Everyone else was already there. Coach Miller stood in front of a flipchart, holding a marker.

"Please take a binder and find a seat," Miller said.

Charlie thought he sounded sort of annoyed.

He didn't waste any time getting started. "Welcome to Team 1," Miller began once Charlie had sat down.

"Please turn to page six in your binder where it says Forechecking Schematics. We'll be working on three different forechecking strategies over camp . . ."

Miller waited for them to find the page. "When you want to slow the game down, or are up against an opponent that is superior offensively, I like to go with the 1–4, which sends one forechecker in deep and four guys spread out in the neutral zone to clog things up. When we need a goal we'll add a forechecker, but the key is the guys in deep must force the puck to one side . . ."

Charlie's head was soon swimming with all the different formations. Next it was backchecking, and then faceoffs. It was hard to follow, but exciting at the same time. This certainly was hockey at a higher level, and he could only imagine how much he was going to learn over the next two weeks.

MISSING IN ACTION

Charlie looked up and saw a Frisbee spinning right for his head. Instinctively, he shot out his hand and snagged the flying disk. Up by the arena doors Scott was laughing away, along with two guys Charlie didn't know.

He took a crossover step forward and let loose. Frisbee was one of his favourite games, and he and Pudge spent hours playing at school. The Frisbee whistled through the air. A tall, thin kid with a black sweatshirt and a shock of red hair reached out and caught it. He waved his hand, pretending it really hurt.

"Yo, Joyce," Scott said when he got closer. "These guys don't believe I'm the best player in camp. You gotta tell them."

"It's true," Charlie said. He paused and added, "Are we talking about hockey?"

That cracked them up. Scott laughed harder than any of them.

"This here is Pete," Scott said. He cupped his mouth and whispered to Charlie, "I call him Pete." He pointed to the other kid. "And this superstar is Jared." Scott held a hand out. "Meet a personal friend of mine, Charlie Joyce," In a loud whisper he added, "Charlie kinda idolizes me. It's a little embarrassing, but what can I do. He cries if I don't let him hang around."

"Thanks for the intro," Charlie said.

"Are you ready for the big squad?" Jared asked him.

The question caught him off guard. He wasn't actually sure if he was. "I guess I am. Miller seems pretty serious. We went over a ton of stuff in the meeting. What about you guys?"

"The basics: forecheck, backcheck, paycheque," Pete said. "No fooling around here. These guys know their stuff. I learned more hockey in that hour than I think I have in my life."

Scott slapped his forehead. "Now you tell me. I was too busy flossing my teeth, and I missed the best hockey talk of all time."

Charlie knew Scott was deadly serious about hockey and that he was only joking. "You won't know what you're doing on the ice, but at least your teeth will be sparkling," he said to keep the joke going.

"Dental hygiene is an important and underappreciated part of the game," Scott said.

The door swung open and Jen came out.

"Shall we get changed for practice, gentlemen? Twenty minutes to get ready." She nodded at Charlie. "Mr. Joyce, I believe you're in this rink. You fellows are in the rink next door.

"I'll catch up with you guys later," Charlie said.

"Come by the room," Scott said. "We can discuss how to get your teeth their whitest — and I should probably review the causes of bad breath." Scott raised his shoulders and looked around like a turtle. "This is kinda awkward. We'll see ya, Joyce."

Charlie waved them off.

"Mr. Joyce, if you please. As much as I like holding doors open . . ."

Charlie gulped and quickly went into the rink. The second he did, the nerves kicked in. This was it — his first Team 1 practice.

* * *

Charlie began dressing extra fast. He wanted to get onto the ice and skate his nerves away. His skates were on before anyone else's. He tossed his shoulder pads on next, and began rooting around in his bag for his elbow pads. Where were they? His bag was so packed with old sweaters and socks he couldn't find them. His mom had told him to clean his bag out, but he'd never bothered. He put his helmet on the bench.

"Let's go, boys," Trevor said, the door closing behind him.

A few players got up.

Charlie continued to hunt for his elbow pads.

Trevor opened the door again. "I wasn't kidding. Move it out."

"Come on, Team 1," one player said as he filed out.

"We're jammin'. Party time, dudes."

Charlie's heart sank. The pads weren't there — impossible. He'd had them yesterday. Had he left them at the other rink? For a second he considered running over, until he thought how idiotic he'd look, not to mention missing part of practice.

Just then the door flung open and Trevor walked in.

"Are you playing today?" Trevor asked him.

"I just gotta tighten my skates."

"Okay," he said uneasily. "Coach Miller is strict about time so . . . I'd hurry."

Charlie said, "Sorry," and pretended to retighten his skates.

Trevor left and Charlie was all alone in the dressing room.

He couldn't play without elbow pads. What could he do? He looked frantically in his bag one last time. All he had was his Rebels shirt and socks. He pulled out the socks, and that gave him an idea — a bit nuts but it was all he could come up with. A minute later, Charlie ran down the corridor and stepped onto the ice — with two hockey socks taped around his elbows for pads.

He didn't have any time to warm up. The whistle blew and Coach Miller pointed his stick to one end.

"On the line, boys. Time to pick up the intensity," Miller said. "The easy practices are over."

Charlie wondered if the man ever smiled.

For the next half-hour Charlie skated harder than he ever had in his life. He used to think his high school teacher and Rebels coach, William Hilton, was tough. Miller was psycho. They hopped and spun and jumped and dove; they tore around the faceoff circles with heads turned up at the scoreboard; they dropped to their knees and did races, the loser having to do twenty push-ups. When Miller finally blew his whistle to signal the end of the skating drills Charlie could hardly catch his breath.

"Here's the drill," Miller announced, and he poked the whiteboard with a marker.

"I'm sure you've done this a hundred times. Continuous alternating one-on-one. Forward in the corner goes around the pylon. When he crosses the blue line, the defenceman comes across and they go one-on-one. Forward then takes a pass from the corner, feeds it ahead to centre and gets a return pass, and then goes one-on-one against the other defenceman."

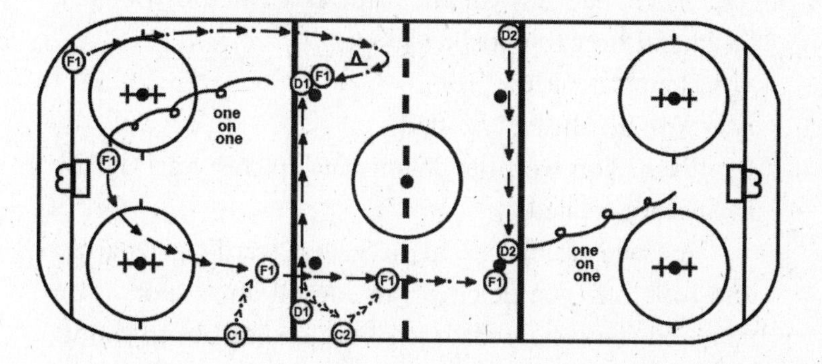

He bashed his stick on the ice. "Defencemen split into two groups. Forwards, I want you all in the right corner."

Charlie joined the forwards. J.C. Savard was a few spots behind, so he drifted back.

"I thought I was in shape," Charlie offered. "My lungs almost exploded."

"I heard from some guys that this is nothing compared to what's coming," Savard replied. "Anyway, congrats for making T1, Charlie."

Charlie reddened. "You too. Guess Terrence Falls and Chelsea did okay." Chelsea was Savard's high school.

"Burnett made it on D, and there's Cameron. He's doing the drill now."

Savard pointed to a swift skating player bearing down on the far goal. Charlie recognized him from Savard's club team, the Snow Birds. He deked to his left, swung the puck across his body to his forehand, and then slipped past the defenceman.

"Sweet move," Charlie said, as Cameron roofed a backhand over the goalie's glove.

They were at the front.

"You go ahead," he said.

"Nah. You won the championship this year. Go for it," Savard replied.

The whistle blew. Charlie gave Savard's pads a tap and took off. The defenceman backed up as soon as he rounded the cone, which left little choice but to shoot. Using the defender as a screen, Charlie got off a howitzer right into the top left corner. That felt awesome, and Charlie was stoked for the next one-on-one as he received a crisp pass from Miller.

Charlie tried going in with one hand on the stick, holding the puck wide with his right hand. Usually, the defenceman went for the puck, and he'd slip it between his legs and step inside. This time the D ignored the puck completely and rode Charlie off to the side.

"Nice play," Charlie said. He wasn't sure but he thought his name was Nathan.

The compliment seemed to have surprised him. "Yeah, thanks," he grunted in return.

As Charlie waited to go again, Trevor skated over to him.

"Hey, Charlie. Careful with that deke. You lose the puck in the neutral zone and your team will get punished on the counter attack. If the D doesn't bite, bounce it outside and at least make sure the puck gets into their end — and take it hard, no soft moves."

He slapped his shin pads and in two seconds was practically at top speed. Charlie marvelled at how effortlessly he skated. Trevor was right, though. These guys knew better than to look at the puck. When his turn came up, he was determined to follow Trevor's advice. He used a spin move at the top of the circle and beat one defender to the outside, only the goalie came out strong and took away the angle and stopped Charlie's snap shot to the short side.

Slogger was defending for the second one-on-one. Charlie took the pass and drifted into centre, faked left with his head, slowed slightly to throw Slogger off, and then broke it outside along the boards. Slogger carved on his edges frantically to head him off.

As he crossed the blue line, Charlie had to slow down to gather the puck, and that let Slogger spin to his left, and his hip just caught Charlie on the inside of his thigh. Charlie bounced off and his right elbow banged against the glass. He kept his feet moving, however, and with the puck sitting about a foot from the boards, Charlie was able to gain the corner and cut towards the goalie, who'd drifted out to the top of the crease. Unfortunately, his elbow was throbbing and, distracted by the pain, he lost control of the puck trying to shovel it stick side with his backhand.

"Next time I won't take it so easy on ya," Slogger joked, as he turned and skated back to centre.

A sick feeling in his gut, Charlie coasted to a stop behind the forward's line. Of course he had to lose his elbow pad and then smash into the boards in the first drill. He gingerly tried to extend his arm — and a shock wave spread up and down his arm.

* * *

The rest of the practice was a nightmare. The pain made it hard to shoot. He'd never been so relieved to hear a coach blow his whistle to signal the end of practice.

In the dressing room the typical horseplay ensued, tape balls whizzing though the air, and the guys dissing each other or bragging about some move or other.

"Zane, how'd it feel getting totally dangled on that one-on-one," a kid named Richard teased.

Zane tilted his chin up. "Shut up, ya goof," he shot back.

Charlie ignored them, struggling to even untie his skates. His right arm was useless. What if it stayed this bad, he wondered. He'd have to go home and lose out on everything. Wouldn't Jake get a kick out of that? He'd probably move up and take his spot.

"How's the arm, bud?" Trevor looked down at him with obvious concern.

"It's kinda hurting. Banged it . . . during practice."

"I thought you got dinged up a bit. You seemed to have trouble carrying the puck. Why don't you drop by the trainer's room? It's down the hall to the right. I'll get you some ice." He hesitated and said quietly, "Do you need some help getting undressed?"

He did — but no way he'd let the others see that! "I'm good. I'll see you in a sec."

Slowed by the elbow, he was the last player out. He walked to the trainer's room and knocked on the door.

"Come in."

Trevor held a plastic bag full of ice. "Sit on this table and let me look it over." He started probing the elbow with his fingers.

"Looks like a fairly nice bruise," Trevor mused. "Weird place to get hurt, though. Your elbow pad must have shifted, 'cause it's usually well protected there. Are your pads too small?"

Charlie flushed and lowered his eyes. This was going to sound lame. "I . . . I lost my elbow pads somehow. Don't know . . . maybe at the last practice."

"You didn't have elbow pads at practice?" Trevor practically shouted.

Charlie smiled weakly. "I wrapped some socks around my arm. Guess it wasn't that effective."

Trevor's mouth scrunched to one side. "Not the smartest thing to do. Don't think you did any serious damage, fortunately. Ice your elbow on the way back to the dorm and I'll bring some more ice for tonight. Might be uncomfortable tomorrow, but you'll live."

He handed the bag of ice over, then snapped his fingers and pointed at him like he was holding a gun. "Check the lost and found. It's by the front doors. Guys are always losing stuff. It's amazing anyone shows up with equipment on at all."

"Sure. Thanks, Trevor. I'll go right now."

"If you don't find anything, let me know and I'll see about hunting down an extra pair."

Charlie thanked him again. He pressed the ice bag against his elbow. The cold felt good. The lost and found was right by the door. Like Trevor had said, there was tons of stuff. A hockey sweater was draped across the top. He tossed it aside — and had to stop himself from yelling out loud. Two elbow pads were sitting on top. He picked them up to take a closer look. That was weird. They looked like his. He looked closer, and had to shake his head twice before accepting that they were his. How had he lost them?

Talk about luck.

He adjusted the ice bag in his hand — well, maybe not that lucky.

At least he had all his equipment again. He raced back to the dressing room and popped his elbow pads into his bag.

OBSTACLE ILLUSION

Charlie thrust his fist into the pouch of his sweatshirt and pulled his hood up. Nick and Scott had their hoods up too.

"This wind is brutal," Charlie said. "Aren't summers supposed to be warm?"

"Can't believe we had to go for a jog at nine in the morning," Nick said.

They entered a forest.

Scott rubbed his stomach. "I'm starving. You think we're going for a picnic?"

Charlie was slightly ahead of his friends, and saw what was next. "I see an obstacle course in our future, dudes."

They gave a mock cheer.

Tweet.

"Run it in, gentlemen," Jen yelled. "Welcome to the obstacle course. I trust you enjoyed your run this morning." A few guys answered with a chorus of boos. Jen arched an eyebrow and continued. "Please divide into two groups — one on the right and the other on the left. We'll go continuous on the course until I see you've worked up a sweat." She pulled her hat down close to her eyes "So let's go hard. It's good for you." No one laughed at her joke, and she sighed. "I suppose it is a touch early for humour. But this is going to be great, I promise; and if I'm in a good mood, we might have a challenge match between the teams."

Jen blasted her whistle and the two guys in the front took off, Corey being one of them. Scott was joking around with Pete and Jared. Jake was holding court with Zane and a few guys from Teams 1 and 2. Charlie decided to take a page from their book. He'd be with these guys for two weeks, and the least he could do was try to make some friends. Behind him a short, broad-shouldered guy was staring off into the forest, a left winger named Richard.

"How'd the run go?" he said.

Richard turned slowly towards him. "It went."

"Hard to get motivated so early in the morning."

"I guess."

"Were you here last year?"

"No."

"Wonder what the course is like."

"We'll find out."

Richard looked away, ending the conversation. How did Scott and Jake do it? That was painful.

Tweet!

"Mr. Joyce, it's your turn," Jen said sternly.

He took off like a shot, high stepping through a

series of car tires. Next he had to run across a long log about a metre above the ground, followed by a water jump and a series of hurdles, which led to a four-metre-high wall. A rope hung in front. Charlie grasped the rope and hauled himself up and over using his feet against the wall as leverage. After the wall there was another series of tires, a rope bridge, a long tube to crawl through, and finally three walls that went up to his shoulders.

He'd just clambered over the last wall when Trevor yelled out, "How's the elbow?"

Charlie waved back. "It's stiff, but I've been icing it non-stop and it feels way better."

Trevor flashed a thumbs-up, and Charlie ran back to the start; and as Jen had said, it was fun. Charlie enjoyed doing the course, and so did the other guys. There was no lack of laughing and joking around before long.

Jake got the biggest reaction when he headed down the course walking on his hands and he tried to continue on his hands through the tires. He ended up wiping out, of course. Even Charlie had to admit it was funny. Jake wasn't the same kid here. It was weird. The Jake he knew was the guy who'd been laughing when Zane challenged him to a fight. So who was the real Jake Wilkenson?

Jen held up her hand. "Organize yourselves into your teams. I want Team 1 on the left and Team 3 on the right. Time for the run off. Teams 2 and 4 will go next. Winners of each race go again for the championship. The champs get a prize — and trust me, you'll want it."

No one seemed too happy about the prospect of another run. Charlie was always up for a race, but he joined his Team 1 teammates in complaining, so as not to seem uncool. Corey was first up for Team 3. He was staring forward intently, knees bent, flexing his fingers slowly.

Jen blew the whistle, sending Corey charging down the course. Charlie was fourth in line, behind Savard. Burnett had led off for Team 1 and returned with the lead, Corey thundering after him. Everything seemed like such a struggle for the guy. The lead grew with each runner, so by the time Charlie tagged Savard's outstretched hand, he had a half-course lead. The rest of the race was a formality. As his teammates celebrated, Charlie noticed Corey off to the side, hunched over.

"So how are ya making out?" he said.

Corey straightened abruptly. "Oh . . . hi." He growled and kicked at the ground with the toe of his shoe. "Team 3's such a joke. They don't even put in an effort — bunch of babies. Why'd I even bother running? Still can't believe I'm on Team 3. Can you?"

"Maybe they want to give some other players a chance. You'll move up, I'm sure."

Corey's head jerked up. "You think I will? Do you really? When?"

Charlie was taken aback. "Um . . . like . . . I'm not sure. Soon."

Corey's expression grew worried. "Lot of competition up the middle. Savard can play, and I hear that

Wilkenson guy is a stud too. There's talk of him moving up . . . and . . . and . . . you're in there too. Not many spots."

Tweet.

"Teams 2 and 4 are up," Jen announced. "Winner takes on Team 1."

Corey didn't seem like he had anything else to say. Charlie cleared his throat. "I'm gonna watch this race . . . see how my friends do."

Corey barely nodded. "I'm gonna go up the course and watch the next race — and good luck in the finals."

This race was closer. Pete was Team 4's first runner, and he tore the course apart. Scott kept the lead, but then Team 2 closed the gap slowly. The two teams were practically even when the last runners left. Jake was anchor for Team 2, and he won the sprint back to the starting line for the win. His teammates gave him a huge cheer.

"Team 2 is True," Jake chanted, as a few others joined in.

"I need Team 1 and 2 on the line for the run off. Let's go," Jen said.

"Same order as last time," Zane ordered.

No one questioned him. Charlie wondered when he became captain, but didn't say anything. He lined up behind Savard.

"Let me in here," Charlie heard Jake say. "We're old friends. It'll be nifty to run against him. Don't you think, Charles?"

Charlie didn't take the bait and pretended he hadn't

heard. He clenched his fists and readied himself. He'd show Jake what Charlie Joyce could do.

Jen's "Go!" brought his attention back to the race. Team 1 got off to a quick start. When Savard returned Charlie had a ten metre lead. He knew Jake was fast, so he pushed himself hard. He made it through the tires and over the water jump in good order, and then raced to the wall.

His rope was gone! He looked around frantically. He couldn't climb a four metre wall without a rope. He reached for the Team 2 rope.

"Get lost, Joyce. That's mine." Jake was steaming towards him.

"Where's my rope?"

Jake screwed his eyes shut and shook his head. "Not my problem," he snarled.

Jake tried to pull the rope away, but Charlie held firm.

"Let go, Joyce, and get out of my way," Jake threatened.

"Since when is it your rope," Charlie said.

"Since it's on my side."

"But there's only one rope. Where's the other one?"

Trevor came running over. "What's going on, guys?" he asked.

"Nothing, other than he's cheating," Jake said, nodding towards Charlie. "He cut me off and took my rope." He tugged on it again.

"Charlie, what's up?" Trevor asked.

"I was in the lead, and when I got to the wall there

was only one rope, so I figured that was the one I had to use. Then Jake came and tried to rip the rope out of my hands . . ."

"You're such a liar it hurts," Jake interrupted.

Trevor looked at them both, and then went behind the wall. The other rope came flying over. "I think I found it," Trevor said.

By this time, Jen and a few other players had come down from the starting line to see what the yelling was about.

"Trevor, why did you end the race?" she demanded.

"I didn't. These two were wrestling over the rope."

Charlie suddenly realized he was still holding on to it. He let go as if it were burning his hands.

"Why'd you do that?" she asked them both.

"Ask him," Jake said. "This is my rope. It's on Team 2's side. He cut me off and wouldn't let me climb the wall."

Charlie tilted his head to one side. "Yes, Jake. I deliberately threw myself in front of you."

Scott and Nick laughed openly. Corey pushed his way to the front.

Jake's eyes were blazing now. "The guy took my rope because I was totally gaining on him. I was about to pass him — and he pulls this junk." He threw the rope against the wall. "I know it's just a stupid race — but it's bogus when someone cheats."

"This was supposed to be fun," Jen said. She sounded irritated. "Why did you take Team 2's rope?" she asked Charlie.

"When I got here there was only one rope."

"Team 1's rope got flipped to the back of the wall," Trevor explained.

Jen pointed at Charlie. "Who went ahead of you?" she asked.

The entire camp was now crowded around.

"That was me," Savard said. "I'm positive the rope was on the right side. Positive. I remember throwing it back. I was paranoid about it so I made sure."

Everyone started to talk at once. Jake crossed his arms and stared with a cocky grin at Charlie.

That was the Jake he knew — the Mister Friendly act didn't fool him. He was lying to get him in trouble, and he thought it was funny. While Charlie fumed, Jen and Trevor moved off to the side.

"I think Team 2 has to be the winner," Jake said. "Joyce took our rope. Open and shut case." Charlie saw Trevor say something to Jen and she shook her head.

"We need to get back," Jen said to them. "You can grab a snack from the cafeteria, and then it's time for practice. It's only a silly race . . . but . . . it looks like Charlie did interfere with Team 2's rope. I have no choice but to declare Team 2 the winner, and they will receive their prize. At the same time, let's all forget about this, and I hope no one will harbour any grudges. Again, it's just a race."

The Team 2 players let out a huge roar and a bunch of guys clapped Jake on the back and shoulders. Markus raised Jake's arm over his head like a boxer who'd won a fight.

"So who wants to run back?" Jen asked cheerfully.

A chorus of "No"s answered her.

"Excellent. Then let's all run back together. Follow me," she said laughing, before setting off at a fast clip.

Charlie followed along, trying to figure things out. It might have been the Team 2 player who ran with Savard. He'd have been behind, and it would have been easy for him. He tried to remember who that was. It came to him in a flash. "Nathan," he practically shouted. A few guys looked at him as if he'd lost his mind. He didn't care. It made perfect sense now. Nathan was the culprit, and Charlie bet Jake had put him up to it. So now he had three guys to worry about — Jake, Zane and Nathan, and maybe he could add Markus to the list. Who else, he wondered? It was easy enough for Jen to say it was only a silly race. All of Team 1 would blame him. How could they not? He'd be the least popular guy on the ice from now on. And it wasn't fair.

"Thanks a lot, teammate," Richard muttered as he ran past, which confirmed what he'd been thinking.

Slogger jogged up beside him. "No worries, dude. Bad decision. Forget about it."

Scott and Nick veered over.

"I don't see how Jake could've done it," Nick said. "It must have been Savard. The rope probably didn't go back over."

"Savard said he was positive he threw the rope to the right side," Slogger interjected.

"I bet Jake was behind it somehow," Scott said.

Charlie kept quiet. If Scott or Nick found out about

Nathan they'd make a big deal about it. He didn't want to draw any more attention to himself. It was enough that he'd figured it out and he could be on his guard. He felt really bad about involving Savard, however. Charlie spotted him running with Burnett and Cameron off to the side. He drifted over towards him.

"Hey, J.C.," he started.

Savard and Burnett stopped their conversation and looked over. Neither seemed too happy.

Charlie felt himself flush. "Sorry about all that . . . garbage. I didn't mean . . . I mean I didn't want . . . I mean I know you didn't forget . . ." He knew he sounded like an idiot, but the right words wouldn't come. "I'm sorry," he blurted.

Savard shrugged. "I doesn't matter — like she said, just a race."

"It's weird, though," Charlie said. "I swear there was only one rope when I got to the wall and . . ."

"Forget about it," Savard said. "It's cool."

He didn't continue, and Charlie felt the growing silence made things awkward. "Okay. Great. I'll catch up with you guys," he said finally.

They nodded, and Charlie dropped back to Slogger, Nick and Scott.

They all looked so serious and worried that Charlie felt doubly bad. He didn't want to bring them down too. "No big deal, guys," he said. "Whenever something sinister happens, Jake's gotta be involved. No mystery there. I'll figure out how he did it if it kills me. I'm not stressing. Besides, there's a good part to all this." He put an arm around Scott's shoulders. "It's snack time."

"I like your thinking, Joyce," Scott said. "I'm so starved I'm gonna need a whole buffet for myself."

"We'd better get there first," Charlie said, "or there won't be anything to eat. Pedal to the metal, dudes."

He accelerated, with his friends hot on his heels.

"Curse everyone who's faster than me," Scott said, breathing heavily.

Charlie heard a few disses as he sped along the trail.

"Why didn't he run like that in the race?"

"Showing off for Jen?"

They actually passed Jen on the path leading to the cafeteria.

"I'm impressed by the effort, gentlemen," she said. "Save some food for me."

"I'd like to," Scott said, "but that's not possible."

Jen laughed and wished them luck.

Together they barged into the cafeteria. Charlie grabbed a pile of trays.

"We won the race that mattered," he said dramatically, tossing the trays Frisbee-style.

"One tray?" Scott said incredulously. "You trying to starve me?" Scott helped himself to three bananas, some cheese and crackers, two pieces of bread, and two yogurt containers — and then added a bunch of grapes and an orange.

"You had breakfast, right?" Slogger asked.

Scott put his forefinger on his chin. "I don't rightly know," he said, as if deep in thought. "I think it would be prudent to eat this in case I forgot."

Charlie was surprised by how hungry he was, and he piled the food on. A nagging feeling bothered him as he ate, however. Dealing with Jake alone was one thing. If Jake had a bunch of guys on his side, they could mess him up in a hundred ways.

He finished his banana. If only Pudge were here. He'd know what to do. Pudge was great at figuring stuff like this out. It would also be cool to have another friend in his corner. He could always count on Scott and Nick. Slogger seemed to be a cool guy too, and Charlie couldn't help but like Corey even though he rubbed those guys the wrong way. Sure he was way too serious about everything, but Charlie could tell he was under intense pressure from his dad to do well at camp. Add in scouts and scholarships, he could understand why he pushed himself so hard.

Which meant Charlie had four guys on his side, against Jake and his gang, and a Team 1 that wasn't very happy with Charlie Joyce at the moment.

Very, very not good — and it could mean serious trouble.

10

DEAD WEIGHT

Charlie pushed his tray away and leaned back. "If I eat any more I'm gonna die."

"So you're not going to finish that apple?" Scott asked.

He rolled it over to Scott. His friend bowed before crunching into it.

Trevor banged a spoon on a table. "Time to award the prize to Team 2 for winning the obstacle course race," he announced.

Charlie's uneasy feeling got a bit worse. He didn't need to be reminded of the race.

"I bet Team 2 doesn't have to go for a run tomorrow," Nick said to Scott.

"Maybe they get to sleep in," Slogger said.

The room quieted down. "Maybe it wasn't the longest race," he said, which got a reaction, "but there was a winner and the prize is amusing, so whatever . . . The grand prize is that each Team 2 member will be piggy-backed to practice. Team 2 now has to decide which team will do the piggy-backing."

A huge cheer went up from some of the guys at Jake's table, all high-fiving, and the hooting and hollering got louder and louder. Jake began chanting, "Team 2! Team 2! Team 2 will destroy you!" and soon all his teammates joined in.

"Huddle up, boys, and pick your team," Trevor said with a laugh. He seemed to think it was all in fun. Charlie had a sinking feeling in the pit of his stomach.

Jake called out, "Give us Team 1," and began chanting "Team 1! Team 1! Team 1!" Soon the cafeteria was in a total uproar.

If they didn't already, the Team 1 players would really hate him now. He honestly thought he'd be sick.

"Gentlemen, before you go, please check the bulletin board," Jen said. "A few players will be moving teams. Think of it as a slight rebalancing. The coaches wanted me to stress that no one is being demoted or punished. They just think a few guys will flourish more on different teams."

After that announcement, the players began to put away their trays and head to the rinks. All of them made sure to check the bulletin board, however; and Charlie noticed some happy faces, and a few sad ones too.

Jake came over to Charlie's table. "My legs are darn tired, Joyce. That obstacle course took a lot out of me. I think I need a lift to the rink. Are you ready?"

With a cocky grin he wandered over to the bulletin board, where Zane and Markus traded high-fives with him. Charlie knew it before he read the new team lists

— Jake Wilkenson, Team 1. He noticed that Corey had moved to Team 2 to take Jake's spot. That would cheer his roommate up at least.

As if on cue, Corey appeared next to him. "Awesome, isn't it?"

He could only assume he was referring to his promotion. "It's great news," he said. "You deserve it."

Corey leaned closer. "I knew it would happen," he said in a confidential tone. "Like you said, it's okay to let some other guys have a chance. I must've sounded totally lame yesterday, worried like an old grandmother. I'll be on Team 1 soon, for sure." He elbowed Charlie, as they made their way outside. "What's this Savard like? Is he really any good? He looks kinda small to me."

"I think he's gotta be one of the best players here," Charlie answered.

Corey's face clouded over. "But he's not that big? I mean, what could he do against me in the corners or in front, right?" He suddenly thrust his hand in his pocket and pulled out his phone. "Hold on a sec, Charlie. It's my dad."

"So I got promoted to Team 2," Corey said. "Yeah, today. This morning. I'm off to practice . . . I'll call you back later."

He put the phone back in his pocket. "I'm gonna run over to the rink — see if I can get on the ice for a bit of a skate around. Catch you later." Corey ran off across the field towards the rink.

"Excuse me, Charlie. Can I have a word with you?" Jen said. Charlie stopped and waited for her. "I don't want to make a big deal out of what happened this morning. But I want to convey to you that issues are piling up: late for training, no form, and now the obstacle course. The coaches discussed moving you down to take some pressure off you, and let you focus more. Do you think that would help?"

Charlie shook his head. It all seemed so unfair. He knew it looked bad, but none of the problems Jen mentioned were really his fault. But she'd think he was a whiner if he said that.

"I'll do better. I know I maybe got off to a slow start . . . being late and stuff." He wondered if she knew about the elbow pads. "I'm good now. I'll be fine."

She peered into his eyes. "You're a nice kid, and we want you to do well. The YEHS is for elite athletes, and if the pressure is bothering you then let me know and I can help. Don't feel like you have to stay on Team 1 to prove something . . ."

Her voice trailed off, and then she waited for him to respond.

"I'm . . . I'm good, like I said. I'm into the rhythm of the camp now. There won't be any more mistakes."

She didn't look entirely convinced. "Okay, Charlie. Why don't you head on out."

Heading out wasn't exactly something to look forward too, but he was happy to end this conversation. He said goodbye and, as he exited, heard shouting and laughing. The piggy-backing must have started.

This wasn't going to be pretty. This was going to be downright ugly!

* * *

A few Team 1 guys had already started towards the rink when he arrived. Team 3 and 4 players had formed a lane and they clapped and dissed the unfortunate piggy-backers as they trucked across the field. Clark, Miller and Binns were watching too, giving good-natured encouragement.

"Mr. Joyce," Jake said grandly. "I've been waiting for my noble steed. Let's make haste. I do not wish to be late for my appointment."

Charlie steeled his nerves and bent down without a word. He wasn't going to give Jake the satisfaction of seeing how embarrassing this was. Jake jumped onto his back.

"Giddy-up, horsey," Jake said gleefully. "Catch up. I wanna win." He slapped Charlie's sides, imitating a jockey.

Everyone was laughing at Jake's antics. It wasn't so comical for Charlie. Jake was a big guy, and once they'd gotten past the onlookers he made sure the ride became painful. The occasional dig of the elbow into his back wasn't the worst part, though. Jake kept up the trash talk the entire way, never letting up for a second.

"Joyce, too bad about the rope. I feel awful about it . . . now that you're my horse and all."

"There was only one rope, I was there first, and I didn't cut you off," Charlie sputtered, as the strain of carrying him became overwhelming.

"You're right. Only, no one else knows that — which is the beauty of situation. The guys on Team 2 love me 'cause I won the race for them. I'm on Team 1 where I belong, and all the Team 1 guys think you're a total cheating doofus — even Savard, he told me. Now I'm not so sure it's cool that we're teammates. But I bet you'll mess up again big time and get sent down. You never know what can happen."

He laughed at that, which confirmed Charlie's suspicions. Nathan had definitely thrown his rope over. When he got to the other side of the field he let Jake drop.

"One day you'll get what you deserve, and I hope I'm there to see it," Charlie said. "And from now on how about we don't actually talk to each other. You're not as interesting as you think."

He brushed past as Zane and Markus came over.

"What did he say?" Zane asked Jake.

"He . . . um . . . he told me . . . He said he has a big booboo on his knee and it's really hurting."

Charlie kept on going. Jake never had to take responsibility for being such a jerk. He was the type of guy who always got away with things. As he reached for the door handle to go into the rink, the door swung open and Slogger stuck his head out.

"Did you survive?" he asked with a cock-eyed grin.

"Not with my pride. How about you?" Charlie said.

"I carried Nathan. Not quite as big as Jake. I got off easy. But I hope we don't lose any more challenges."

Charlie paled. "I guess I'd better apologize to the guys. No one's gonna be too happy to see me."

Slogger looked surprised. "I didn't mean it like

that." His eyes lowered to the floor and then back at Charlie. "Some guys buy Jake's act. I'm not one of them. I'm not buyin' it for one second. The guy is too cool by half. I'll see how tough he is on the ice."

"Jake's an awesome player," Charlie said. "He's probably one of the best players here."

Slogger shook his head. "I don't get you, Charlie. Scott filled me in on the Rebels and your school team, and all the garbage Jake's pulled on you — and then you tell me how great he is."

Charlie had to laugh. "Maybe awesome is going too far. How about barely okay?"

"That sounds more like it," Slogger said, and together they went in.

11

LOSERS WEEPERS

Jen almost ran them over running up the stairs from the dressing rooms. She seemed almost out of breath, and for the first time since Charlie had met her, she looked really angry.

"Sorry, gentlemen. Did you see anyone come down these stairs?"

"Not really," Charlie said. "We just got here." He pointed at Slogger. "We kinda had piggy-back duties."

He expected her to laugh. Stone-faced, she replied, "Spread the word that Coach Miller's Stanley Cup ring is missing. He left it in the coaches' change room this morning . . ." She closed her eyes briefly and with two outstretched hands said, "Are you sure you didn't see anyone? Who came in before you?"

"I came in right before Charlie," Slogger said. "I didn't see anyone — at least I don't remember anyone off the bat."

She groaned slightly. "This is all I needed. Okay. Get dressed."

"Do you want us to help look?" Charlie said.

"No, thank you. You have to get ready." She sprang up the stairs two at a time and walked quickly towards the door.

"You don't think someone would actually steal it, do you?" Charlie asked Slogger. It seemed unbelievable. Steal a Stanley Cup ring! "You could never wear it around, and . . ." He gave his head a shake. It seemed too unreal.

"It would be a totally bold move. I mean, to go into the coaches' room, dig around and take the ring . . . a bold move."

"Miller's gonna totally lose it," Charlie said.

Slogger opened the dressing room door. "Did you guys hear about Miller?" he said. "Jen just told us. Someone stole his Stanley Cup ring."

"That's wack," Simon said. "For real? No way!"

"Where'd you hear that?" Cameron asked.

"Jen told us," Slogger said.

"What's the controversy?" Jake said, as he flopped on the bench by his equipment.

"Jen said someone's ripped off Miller's ring."

Jake's eyes grew big, and he laughed incredulously. "Now that's a big score. How much would a Stanley Cup ring be worth? Thousands, I bet."

"You'd get a ton of money, like twenty thousand dollars," Zane said.

"Not that much, dude," Jake snorted. "Give me a break."

"Yeah . . . well . . . like I care," Zane muttered, and

he went over to open his bag. Slogger sat down as well. Charlie looked around for his bag. The guys continued to talk about the ring. Jake took the lead, speculating on who took it and how he'd sell it without getting caught. Charlie, meanwhile, was feeling ridiculous standing in the middle of the room looking for his equipment. But where was it? He scanned the room again.

"You gonna give us a pep talk, Joyce?" Jake said, finally noticing him.

He laughed, but he knew it sounded nervous and panicky. His equipment was probably in another room. "Maybe later," he said, and he turned and left. As the door closed he heard some guys laughing. He leaned against the wall and closed his eyes. Why didn't he just say his bag wasn't there? He sounded completely lame — and was dissed by Jake yet again.

Staying calm got a lot harder as he searched the other dressing rooms. They'd practiced here yesterday afternoon, so where else could it be? He wandered into the lobby, his mind racing.

Trevor was standing by the vending machines. "Shouldn't you be getting ready?" he said.

Charlie had run out of ideas, and so, trying not to sound too desperate, he said as casually as he could, "I'm sort of looking . . . for my equipment."

Trevor raised one eyebrow and pulled his head back. "I might try the dressing room."

"I did . . . it's not there."

"Where could it be?"

"I wish I knew," he said meekly.

"First Miller's ring, and now this." Trevor raised his arms and let them flop to his sides. "Did you check all the other rooms?" he said quickly.

Charlie nodded.

"Charlie, this is not good. How can you lose your equipment?"

Charlie looked down at the floor.

"I'll help you look," Trevor said softly. "Come on. It has to be here somewhere."

Ten minutes later they'd looked in the coaches' room, the trainer's room, upstairs in an office and even in a storage room that Charlie had never seen. His panic level doubled when the Team 1 players began to file onto the ice. Trevor seemed almost as distressed as Charlie.

"This is bizarre. I have to get ready. I'm doing the warm-up drills for Team 1 today." He looked genuinely upset. "Find Jen and have her help you. Sorry, but I have to get my skates on." He ran back to the coaches' room, leaving Charlie alone in the lobby. Coach Miller swept past him, followed by Jen and Coach Binns. They all looked very, very angry. Halfway down the stairs, Jen whirled and came stomping back to him.

"Precisely why are you standing here when there's a practice, Mr. Joyce?"

"I can't find my equipment."

"How is that possible?"

"I don't know," he said miserably. "Me and Trevor looked all over. I . . . I . . ."

"I bet the ring is in your stupid bag," Jen cut in.

"I didn't take the ring," he said breathlessly.

"I didn't say you did. Sorry. I'm just annoyed." She rolled her neck around once. "Fine. Where did you look?"

Charlie told her, and she closed her eyes and shook her head slowly from side to side. "Well, there's nowhere else. It must be in one of the other rinks. Maybe someone carried it over by mistake."

"Why would someone take my stuff?" he said.

"Do you have a better idea, Mr. Joyce?"

Charlie gulped and said, "No," following Jen outside.

* * *

Head down, and feeling as self-conscious as he ever had in his life, Charlie glided across the ice to join the group of forwards at the far end. Practice was half over. He was still unnerved by the whole thing. Jen had found his equipment in an empty dressing room in Rink 3. It certainly didn't help his nerves when Coach Clark called him over the second he fell into line. He hadn't realized Clark would be running the practice.

"Charlie Joyce, come over here please, and the rest of you, form a semicircle behind me. I want to show you something."

Charlie dutifully skated to the front of the net, dreading what was going to come next.

"I've been told you lost your equipment?" Clark said.

"Somehow it got put in the other rink — sorry," Charlie managed.

The corners of Clark's eyes hardened. "That is very odd," he said slowly.

By this time the other players had gathered around. Much to Charlie's relief, Clark didn't dwell on his misplaced equipment. "I'm sure coach Miller has spoken to you about net presence — although in my day we called it standing in front of the net or screening the goalie. Anyway, I've noticed most of you forwards are remaining stationary, which is allowing the defenceman to establish position.

"Charlie, I want you to be the forward, and I'll be the defenceman." He banged the tip of his stick on the ice about seven feet from the top of the crease. "Stand here and see if you can score. Trevor, you fire a few passes from the corner."

Why did Clark have to pick him? He felt even more self-conscious, not to mention a little awed, actually playing against Clark, a former NHL player. He'd been retired for years, but Charlie had seen him skating around and shooting and the man could definitely still play.

"Let's go, Trevor," Clark said.

Each pass was perfect. Right on Charlie's stick, and not too hard. But each time, Clark knocked his stick, bumped him slightly or poked the puck away. He wasn't even taking advantage of his size. Soon the guys started laughing, which only added to Charlie's embarrassment.

"Okay, Trevor. Hold up," Clark said finally. "You're all laughing — but you all do the same thing. You race to the front of the net because that's what you've been taught, and then you're static. That allows the D to keep the puck away. When I played I loved guys who stood in front like statues. Now this time, Charlie, I want you to move around, and when you feel you have an opening, power hard to a spot, make yourself available for a pass, bend low, and get strong."

Clark said to go, and Charlie faked to his right and charged down low to his left about four feet from the post. Trevor anticipated the move and the puck arrived the second he put on the brakes. Clark extended his stick and push him with his left arm, but Charlie was able to get a shot on net to the short side.

Clark tapped Charlie on the helmet. "Well done. That was perfect. Did you see that, boys? Movement, position, shot. It's that simple. Very difficult to defend without taking a penalty. Let's try once more."

Trevor was to his left, so Clark would expect him to go to that side. Counting on Trevor's skills, and he'd seen plenty of them at work since camp started, Charlie spun to his right, dancing past Clark and took two steps to the far post. The puck saucered onto his stick, and he knifed at it with his forehand. It was one of those miracle shots, when the puck rockets off your stick and you wonder how you did it. The puck nicked the bottom of the crossbar and ricocheted into the net.

Several of the onlookers let out a cheer. Charlie forced himself not to smile too broadly. It would look like he was dissing the coach. Coach Clark didn't seem to mind, however, and slapped his stick several times and held out his glove to Charlie for a high-five.

"Well done — and done to perfection. Did you see that? Movement. Aggression. Purpose. Put the defender under pressure and you'll get your scoring chances. Remember that eighty percent of all goals are scored within ten feet of the net. So ask yourselves all the time: Am I in position to score? Am I in position to screen the goalie? Am I in a position to receive a pass? If you're not, move.

"Trevor, you'll feed the forwards. We'll take turns, forwards trying to get free, defencemen working to stop them."

Charlie was about to join the forwards when Clark called him over.

"That was good effort, Charlie," he said. "I'd like to see more of that. Play with confidence — that's something for you to focus on. You've got the ability, and the jam too, to be a great player. It's lack of confidence that holds you back, and maybe a lack of attention sometimes. I know you've been late to some things and have had some problems with some of the activities. Are you enjoying the camp, Charlie?"

The kindness of the question took him by surprise. He was half expecting to get demoted, especially after speaking with Jen before practice.

He hesitated. "Yeah. Of course. It's been great. I've learned a ton of stuff already. Coach Miller is awesome. And you're right about me standing still. My coach back at Terrence Falls tells me the same thing. Never stop skating in hockey."

Clark seemed to approve. "I like the sound of this coach of yours. Good advice."

Charlie figured he was done. "Thanks," he said, and was about to join the line when Clark added, "Let's keep track of that equipment of yours."

Before Charlie could answer, Clark blew his whistle. "I need a forward and D in front, please," he ordered.

Charlie fell in behind Simon and Gabriel. He'd gotten to know them a little bit since that first practice, although they tended to hang out together and not socialize much with others. They were very, very serious players, and rarely joked around — the complete opposite of Scott and Nick.

Savard and Zane were the first pair up. The shifty centre used his tremendous quickness and soft hands to convert a pass into a goal, and narrowly missed a second. Zane slammed his stick on the ice as two more players took their position.

"What did Clark have to say about you being so late for practice?" Gabriel asked him.

"Where were you?" Simon followed up. "We thought you'd gotten hurt and had gone back to the dorm."

He figured he might as well tell them the truth. "You won't believe, it but I found my equipment at Rink 3. Jen was gonna kill me, I swear. It didn't help that she was beyond mad about Miller's ring."

Simon scowled. "You're having your share of bad luck. That rope thing was crazy."

"Jen's okay, but I don't think she was fair to you," Gabriel said.

Charlie didn't want to rehash that. He had a feeling most of the guys were still mad at him. But it was cool that at least these two guys were giving him the benefit of the doubt.

"Next pair," Clark yelled.

"You're up," Gabriel said, pushing Simon forward.

Charlie considered Clark's advice as he waited for his turn. Confidence. That was a good idea. He'd known the competition would be intense. But he'd done okay — maybe even better than okay. He was still on Team 1, although Jen had made it clear that could change.

He readied himself. From now on Charlie Joyce was going to take it to a higher level — starting with this drill.

"Next."

Charlie took his place in the slot and waited for the whistle.

12

PICKPOCKET

". . . and I want Charlie, Simon and Gabriel as the other line. We only have about ten minutes for a scrimmage — but too much drilling dulls the senses. We need to put some of this stuff into action." Clark blasted his whistle. "Line 'em up, boys."

Simon tapped Charlie on the shin pads. "Let's wheel and have some fun."

"Sounds good to me," Charlie said. He could tell Simon loved to play, and that he was never happier than when a coach announced a scrimmage, even a short one. He knew because he was the same way.

"This is our puck," Gabriel said, joining them as they skated to centre for the faceoff. "Careful of neutral zone turnovers — and we go hard on the forecheck."

Savard's line was out against them. Richard was on the left, and a kid named Tan was the right winger. The two lines were evenly matched. He knew all about Savard, and Charlie vowed to watch him all over the ice. Richard was a tough-minded player, kind of like Simon, although maybe not quite as skillful. Tan was a bit on the small side, but his speed was a killer, easily a match for Gabriel.

Trevor dropped the puck hard and it bounced off the ice. Their sticks clashed and on the rebound Savard was able to swipe it to the boards with his forehand. Richard and Simon were on it, but Simon got there a touch faster and he flipped it back to his D, who rifled a pass across to the right defenceman. Charlie anticipated the play and curled deeply in the neutral zone and cut up just as the defenceman took the pass. The puck barely touched his stick before it was on Charlie's — a perfect pass. Savard reached in to head him off just as Simon came off the wall at a 45-degree angle. Charlie took a step and snapped a pass. He had to put it slightly behind him to avoid Savard's stick, but Simon kicked it up to his stick easily.

The right defenceman stepped up to force him, and Simon flipped the puck up high into the near corner. Gabriel let Simon continue on to force the play, and he glided in behind to add pressure. Charlie hovered up high, worried about leaving Savard alone. Simon went in hard and jarred the puck loose. Gabriel jumped on it and went behind the net. With the puck in his possession Charlie switched into offence mode and moved into the slot. Miller had told him to be confident, so . . .

The left defenceman charged at Gabriel in the corner. The left winger backhanded the puck along the boards. Charlie swept in to retrieve it, and immediately felt Savard's presence. With not much choice, Charlie moved it back towards the blue line slowly. Out of the corner of his eye, he saw Simon creep in behind the net. They were set up for the cycle. Charlie didn't hesitate. He backhanded it to Simon, who took it to the other side, where Gabriel moved in to help out. Three times Charlie had the puck behind the net or along the boards, and each time he chopped it down low to a waiting linemate. It was grinding hockey, and all three forwards took some punishment, but it was also satisfying to keep the puck for so long. Finally, Charlie spotted his right defenceman open at the point and he snapped a carom pass to him along the wall.

Simon immediately crashed the net. Charlie remembered Clark's advice and the drill they'd done. Keep those feet moving, Joyce, he said to himself, and so rather than wait for the shot he charged to the slot. The defenceman faked the shot and passed it across to his partner, who let it rip from about five feet inside the blue line. Simon offered himself as a screen, so Charlie decided to camp out at the top of the crease to the goalie's left. The goalie ducked low and dropped into his butterfly. The puck bounced off his left pad and ricocheted off Charlie's skate. For a second he thought he had the short side open, until Savard lifted his stick momentarily and the left defenceman swept the puck out of danger into the corner.

Richard swooped in neatly and drove up ice. Exhausted after a hard shift, the right winger dumped it in and changed up, as did all the players on Charlie's side. On the bench, Charlie took several deep sips of water, and passed the bottle to his linemates.

"Good effort," he said. "We had the puck the entire shift. We'll put one in next time."

Simon sent a small stream of water onto the ice in a high arc. "I should've tipped that shot. Just missed it."

"The D got his stick between my legs and got me off to the perimeter before the shot. I was useless. As least Charlie got close to the puck," Gabriel said.

Charlie thought all three of them had played great. Simon and Gabriel had worked like monsters on the boards, cycling the puck, and the shot was right on. If Savard had been half a second slower, Charlie would have scored. They were so hard on themselves, but it was in a good way. It fired him up to work even harder. He turned his attention to the game. The play raged back and forth at a tremendous pace. He found himself getting antsy watching — he had to get back out there!

Soon enough the centre signalled a change and Charlie hurled himself over the boards. Jake had the puck in his own end, curling in front of his net, moving slowly. Charlie went straight at him, figuring he'd be tired at the end of a long shift. Jake saw him and looked to his right to pass to his winger, so Charlie held his stick out to intercept. That changed Jake's mind and he swerved back to his left, one hand on the stick, driving hard for open ice.

Charlie had the advantage of being well rested, and he was able to double back and swing his stick as Jake crossed the blue line. He caught a piece of the puck, and it hopped over Jake's stick. The two defencemen had spread out wide to give Jake an outlet, which meant Charlie had an unobstructed lane to the net. Charlie kicked it forward with his right foot and brought the bouncing puck under control by tapping the top of the puck with the bottom of his blade.

The goalie immediately came out, crouched low, his glove held out wide a little over waist level. His name was Theodore; lightning quick and fearless, he loved to challenge shooters on breakaways, and he was very difficult to beat on a deke. His only weakness was his height. Not the tallest kid, he could be beaten upstairs. Both defencemen were charging to close the gap, so he didn't have too much time. Charlie dragged the puck behind his back foot, feinted to his backhand and then took a step to his left as if he wanted to deke stickside. The goalie backed up, ready to drop into the butterfly.

"Perfect," Charlie thought. He pulled the puck towards his skates with the tip of his stick and snapped a forehand to the top corner. The goalie had given him too much net, and the puck flew over his arm and in.

Charlie curled back to his end, stick across his knees. It was only a scrimmage, so he wasn't going to make a big deal over a goal, although it felt awesome to pick Jake's pocket. In fact, he saw Clark speaking to Jake against the boards. Jake was looking at the ice, nodding occasionally. Maybe that would shut him up.

Gabriel and Simon held out their hands and he high-fived them.

"That's the way to forecheck," Gabriel said. "Let's keep getting on them real quick."

Charlie rapped his shin pads with his stick and lined up for the draw. Savard came out for Jake.

"That's almost two goals in two shifts," Savard said to Charlie. "Take it easy. You're making us look bad."

That was typical J.C. He always made it seem like everyone else was amazing and he was just an average player. Charlie had played against him enough this past year to know he was capable of scoring two goals on any shift if the other team wasn't careful.

"This time Gabriel's gonna score, so don't worry about me," Charlie said, to his right winger.

"I thought I was gonna get two?" Gabriel said.

"Can we play some hockey already?" Richard growled.

Clark obliged, dropping the puck. Savard showed he was ready by winning the draw back to the right D. Charlie scolded himself for losing the draw so easily. He hadn't been focused and Savard made him look bush.

He forechecked, one hand on his stick to take away the inside lane, waving it side to side slightly to make it harder to pass. The defenceman was smart and only faked the inside move, hitting Savard with a pass in the seam about six feet from the boards. Simon left his man to force Savard, who deftly flicked the puck over Simon's stick to Richard. The burly winger took three powerful strides over centre and dumped it into the opposite corner for his left winger.

Charlie hustled to cover Savard. But he wasn't the easiest guy to keep in check. He took off without warning to the left side and before Charlie could get there the puck was on his stick, courtesy of a sharp pass from the winger who had outraced the defender to the corner. Savard threw on the brakes at the hash marks, with his back to Charlie, as his teammates streamed into the zone. Charlie felt good, however. He had Savard trapped against the wall, and there wasn't much he could do.

He couldn't have been more wrong. Savard whirled towards the blue line with the puck on his forehand and snapped a pass down low to the left winger who had managed to sneak past the defenceman. The winger one-timed it across the crease to Richard, and the puck was in before Charlie or any of his teammates could move.

Charlie slapped the ice with his stick. "We were supposed to score," he said to Savard in admiration.

"That wouldn't be fair," he replied good-naturedly, as he skated to the net to congratulate Richard.

It was a different Charlie Joyce who lined up for the faceoff this time. Corey had said it all: You can't take a shift off. This time he blocked Savard's stick, and knocked the puck with his forehand to the boards close to his right defenceman.

In a repeat of the previous play, Savard forechecked and Charlie took a short pass from his defencemen. He spun and headed up ice, crossing the red line before firing it into the corner for Simon. He corralled the rolling puck and ringed it around the wall to Gabriel. Charlie followed the play intently, looking for an open seam. Gabriel didn't hesitate. He took the puck, drove hard back behind the net, and cut into the front of the net past a startled defencemen. The goalie dropped to his knees and pressed up against the post.

That wasn't a problem for Gabriel. He pulled the puck back a fraction and flipped it up under the cross-bar, before taking a late hit. He spun to the ice on his knees and popped back up seemingly in one motion.

Charlie marvelled at his right winger's skills. What a goal — truly worthy of the highlight reel. As they lined up for the faceoff, Charlie noticed Savard was dead serious for the draw this time, as were all the players. Lesson learned by everyone: don't take a shift off or the puck's in your net.

Charlie leaned into Savard and inched his stick forward in anticipation of Clark dropping the puck.

13

STICKS AND STONES

Corey's phone rang. The door to the bathroom flung open, and he came bounding across the room to grab it from the nightstand next to his bed.

"Hol' on a sec, Da . . ." he struggled to say, his mouth full of toothpaste. He returned to the bathroom to spit and rinse his mouth.

Scott and Nick came into the room. "Is there a Joyce in the house?" Scott called out.

"You dudes ready to play?" Charlie asked.

Corey had spent most of last night talking about the capture the flag game they were playing this morning.

"The winning team gets a cup," he told Charlie, "and the other guys gotta clap you off the field; and they have to wait for you to eat breakfast. It's totally awesome. And last year I snagged the flag for the win and the guys carried me on their shoulders. It was a total riot."

He had laughed about that for what seemed like forever. But he didn't look too happy now as he came out of the bathroom and tossed his phone onto his bed. His mood changed instantly when he saw Charlie's friends. "I'm totally stoked for capture the flag," he said to them. "Did I tell you I found the flag last year to win it?" he asked Charlie.

Charlie nodded.

"I did not know that," Scott said. "Please, tell us all about it."

The last thing Charlie wanted was another play-by-play of how Corey had nabbed the flag.

"We'll be late if we don't get going," Charlie interjected. "I don't need Jen busting me for a punctuality infringement again."

"Those are big words, Charlie," Nick said. "Have you been taking your smart pills?"

"You can get smart pills?" Scott exclaimed.

"You can," Nick said, in a sad voice. "But unfortunately, you need to have a brain first or the pills don't work."

Scott's shoulders sagged. "I should've gone to the Wizard of Oz for some brains when I had the chance."

"Why didn't you?" Nick asked.

"It's a long story. There were these flying monkeys, and a tin guy, and a dog, and this nice girl with an awesome voice . . ."

They all headed to the front doors.

Corey tugged on Charlie's shoulder to hang back. "Your friends are good guys, but they're kinda weird, aren't they?" Corey whispered to Charlie.

"You have no idea," Charlie said.

* * *

It was still early and there was a chill in the air. Charlie was a touch cold and he bounced lightly on his toes to stay warm.

"Didn't your mommy tell you to go to the washroom before you left the house?"

Jake exchanged a high-five with Zane.

"Good timing, dude," Markus chimed.

Charlie stopped bouncing.

"What's going to be your excuse for cheating at capture the flag — a weak bladder?" Jake continued.

The guys around Jake laughed loudly. Charlie rolled his eyes.

Jake kept going. "Heard about your lost equipment. Maybe you should tie a string from your bag to your finger so you don't lose it again."

Charlie bit his lip to help control his temper. Jake would love for him to say something. Then he'd diss him back and all the guys would laugh some more.

"You must be all happy and giggly 'cause you scored a goal in scrimmage yesterday. Mommy would be so very proud of her little Charlie-Warlie."

Charlie caught Slogger's eye. Then he noticed that Simon and Gabriel were watching him too. Nick and Scott were also staring at him intently, and Savard, Burnett, and Cameron were quietly looking on. Were they waiting for him to respond? He took a deep breath. All camp he'd ignored Jake as best he could, figuring he shouldn't lower himself to his level. His instincts told him maybe he'd let things go too far without standing up for himself. He ignored the growing knot in his stomach.

"You're not too chatty today, Charles," Jake continued. "Run out of lame things to say?" Zane snickered behind him. Jake snapped his fingers. "I have an idea. Why don't you regale us with the tale of how I pounded you out this season?" He turned to Zane. "Unfortunately, my good buddy got so scared after our tussle he didn't play for a month. Ain't that right, Char?"

The fight was a low point in the season for Charlie. He'd just been cross-checked by Jake and was totally out of it. After the fight, Jake had acted like he was the heavyweight champion of the world.

"Why don't you tell the guys who won the championship this year," Charlie said quietly.

He snorted. "Worst team in the league gets totally lucky, and you act like you won the Stanley Cup."

"But the Rebels did win — and the Wildcats did lose; and I think you play for the Wildcats. Doesn't that make you . . . I don't know . . . a loser?"

Jake's eyes narrowed. "We were winning until the ref gave the game to you."

"I think you mean you were winning until you quit on your team."

About half the camp was listening to them now.

"On second thought, I think you talk too much," Jake snarled, stepping towards him.

Charlie had no intention of fighting. "You're like a bad video game," he said. "Same thing over and over. We all know that when the pressure's on, you quit. You quit our high school team in the semifinals, and you quit against the Rebels in the championship game."

"I think that makes him a quitter," Scott said to Nick.

"It all adds up," Nick said.

A buzz rose amongst the players. Charlie guessed that tidbit of information surprised them big time. Jake acted like the toughest guy at camp — but tough guys don't quit.

"Attention, everyone," Jen yelled.

That broke things up and they all turned towards her and Trevor. She waved red and blue cloths over her head, and dropped a canvas bag to the ground.

"As those of you who've been here before know," Jen said, "the only thing bigger than the Challenge Game is the Capture the Flag Cup." Trevor held the cup over his head, which garnered a loud cheer.

She continued. "We're going to do something a bit different this year. Instead of matching the teams against each other, we've divided the camp into two groups — Blue and Red." She pointed to a pile of pinnies on the ground. "I'll call out the Blue team first and you'll take the south end. Trevor will help organize you. Grab a pinny when your name's called and head down there. As you can see, in each end zone there's a banner with your team colour." Jen held up the two bands of cloth. "These are your flags. You can hide them in the forest, but they must be clearly visible from at least one direction. Hiding your flag completely will result in automatic disqualification.

"I'm standing on the centre line. Tackle an opposing

player on your side of the field and that player must go to jail. You'll see a big circle around the banners in chalk — that's jail. Jailed players can be freed if a team member runs through the chalked circle."

"Do you have to run through it or can you just put a foot inside?" someone asked.

"What do you think, Trev?" she asked.

Trevor scrunched his face to the side. "One foot inside is good," he declared dramatically.

Jen laughed. "One foot it is. First team to find the other team's flag and carry it back to his own side is the winner. The boundaries are the rinks on my left and the ridge of the escarpment in the forested area, overlooking the ravine on my right. Careful of the forest. There are fallen branches and logs everywhere and the escarpment is very steep. We have two hours, so we might have a few games. But the cup goes to the winner of the first game. Good luck."

"Jen and I will be judging," Trevor said, "so keep to the rules. Just like in football, if your knee touches the ground, you've been tackled."

Jen began calling out names. Charlie got called early for the Blue team, and he was glad to hear Slogger, Gabriel and Simon were also on his team. Scott and Nick were Red, unfortunately.

"Charlie, I don't want you crying and having a tantrum when we win," Scott said. "It's so embarrassing, and it reflects very badly on me since everyone knows I'm your mentor and idol."

"I'll try to keep it together," Charlie said, forcing

himself to joke around. He was still preoccupied with his run-in with Jake.

"And let's remember to just have fun — and use your words," Nick said.

"And no put-downs," Scott said emphatically.

"You're not the boss of me," Nick replied.

Slogger was laughing his head off. "Let's get away from these dudes. They're a bad influence."

Corey came over to Charlie with his fist extended. He wore a red pinny. Charlie punched his fist. "You guys stoked?" Corey said to Scott and Nick. "We gotta smoke these guys."

"Yeah, absolutely," Scott said slowly. "We just gotta . . . smoke them — big time."

"If we don't, then . . . we won't have . . . smoked them," Nick said.

"I'll see you boys down at the banner," Corey replied, oblivious. "You'll see me running down the field with the blue flag."

He slapped Charlie and Slogger and ran off, high-fiving Trevor as he passed him.

"I have to admit I think he wants this more than me," Scott said.

"Gentlemen, could you please get to your team ends. We want to get started," Jen said to them.

"I'd like to apologize for my friends," Scott said solemnly. "They simply won't listen. I pleaded with them to go to their respective banners, but they refused. The problem is they want me to tell them more stories about my hockey career, and of course, how I play the game and strategy and all that. I guess it's my fault for being so interesting."

Jen slung her arm across Scott's shoulders. "Perhaps you could show some leadership skills and get going yourself, Mr. Slatsky."

"That was my plan, except —"

Charlie intervened. Scott could go on forever. "Jen, order him to go, or this'll only get worse. Trust me."

She nodded at him. "Now that's good advice." She pointed at Scott and Nick. "You two — get going. Red needs you."

"Did you hear that?" Scott gasped. "We're needed!"

"Heigh-ho!" Nick sang.

"Heigh-ho!" Scott replied.

"Heigh-ho . . . Heigh-ho . . . it's off to Red we go!" they sang in unison.

Simon and Gabriel waved Charlie and Slogger over.

"Hey, Trevor," Gabriel called out. "Us four will be an attacking unit. Okay?"

Trevor nodded, and turned back to sorting out the rest of the Blue team. Charlie surveyed the scene while everyone waited for the game to begin. The forest wasn't that wide because of the escarpment, but it did offer the only cover.

"Maybe we should slip off into the forest before the game starts," Charlie whispered, "and we can use the cover to get deep into Red's end before they know we're coming."

"Charlie, that's sneaky, devious and underhanded," Slogger said. "So let's do it."

Simon and Gabriel nodded, both grinning broadly. Charlie walked behind the crowd of Blue players milling around their banner, and when he thought the Red players couldn't possibly see them he snuck into the forest, with Slogger, Simon and Gabriel close behind.

"Attack mode, Zebra Squad," Charlie said. "Move out."

14

BATTERED AND BRUISED

All four boys ran off, although it wasn't easy with all the trees, brush, fallen logs and branches. Some of the trees were huge, especially the evergreens. They wound their way as best they could, hugging the hillside to keep out of sight.

"Zebra Squad," Charlie hissed. "Danger at twelve o'clock."

Two Red defenders were wandering through the woods towards them. At that moment, Jen blew her whistle. The game was on.

Charlie and Slogger ducked behind a tree. Unfortunately, Simon and Gabriel only found a scraggly bush to hide them. They lay on the ground, but the Red players spotted them.

"Over here," one of them cried, and three more Reds came bounding over.

Simon and Gabriel scrambled to their feet and ran towards the field, with the Red defenders hot on their heels. Charlie pulled on Slogger's arm.

"We can sneak along the ridge. They'll be too busy with those guys."

"Proceed with caution, dude. We're in enemy territory."

Charlie grinned and together they continued along, looking closely for Red's flag.

Off in the distance Charlie heard someone yell, "You're going to jail!" which got his adrenaline going.

"Let's regroup behind those bushes and figure out where the flag's hidden."

They wasted no time throwing themselves behind a huge evergreen tree.

"We need some walkie-talkies to communicate with Headquarters," Charlie joked.

"I'm sure they'd be impressed that we found a tree to hide behind," Slogger laughed.

Charlie peered through the branches and spotted Simon and Gabriel being led by three defenders. "Looks like they captured two members of Zebra Squad."

"I think our mission is clear," Slogger said.

Charlie pretended to talk into a walkie-talkie. "Delta, Delta, this is Zebra Squad. We're attempting a rescue before capturing the flag. Over."

"What did they say?"

"Couldn't hear them. Signal is jammed."

They crawled along the ridge, dropping to the ground if a Red player came too close and, using the trees as cover, wound their way closer and closer to Red's jail. Charlie got to within ten metres, using another big evergreen as cover. Slogger was a little ways back, hidden behind the trunk of a massive maple. Four of their teammates were in the jail, including Simon and Gabriel. Five defenders were guarding and taunting their prisoners.

"You guys managed to stay free for about ten seconds. Enjoying the game?"

"Check out this dude — I think he's crying."

"And this one's wet his pants."

They laughed uproariously.

Charlie held up three fingers and Slogger nodded. He counted down, and then they both charged the jail. Charlie, who had been closer, got there first.

"Freedom — Blue team!" he screamed.

"Where'd he come from?" a defender yelled, scrambling to his feet.

The prisoners scattered in every direction, as the Red defenders charged after them.

"Zebra Squad — meet at midfield," Simon yelled.

"There's that Joyce guy," a Red player said. "After him!"

Charlie saw Slogger race to the open side of the field. "Go for it, Slogger! I'll see you in friendly territory," he yelled, opting for the forest instead.

It was tough going, and because he was running so fast, he came close to wiping out a bunch of times. His daredevil tactics worked, however, and soon he managed to put some distance between himself and the Red players.

"We'd better go back to the jail," he heard one guy say.

"Yeah. He ain't worth the hassle," another said.

With a sense of relief, Charlie slowed up. He figured the Blue end was about twenty metres further, and then he could safely leave the forest. Charlie ambled to his right, looking around for an opening.

Just then, he felt a hard thump in the stomach, and his breath left him. Ambushed! The defender wrapped a pair of enormous arms around him in a bear hug and tackled him to the ground, landing full on top, winding Charlie again. The defender was huge and Charlie couldn't move.

"Yo! Come over, guys. I got Joyce."

Just his luck to be captured by Zane. "You can get off me now," Charlie gasped.

Zane answered by pressing Charlie's head into the ground. A pine cone dug into his forehead. Then, "Get up slowly," Zane ordered.

Charlie crawled to his knees. Zane jerked him to his feet.

"Chill, dude. It's just a game," Charlie said.

The other defenders who'd been chasing him had doubled back when Zane called them.

"Zane, awesome tackle," Richard said.

"You're down, Joyce," the other kid said.

Charlie was still catching his breath.

"Aw, poor little guy's upset. Can anyone get this baby some juice?"

"That's funny, dude. Joyce needs some juice."

"Hey. Let's call him Juice," Richard said gleefully.

"Call him Apple Juice," Zane said, which caused an uproar of laughter.

"Into jail, Apple Juice!"

Charlie felt like he was back in grade three. These guys were so lame. It was irritating to get caught, but he was sure Zebra Squad would set him free in no time. The tackle was hard to take, though. Punching a guy in the stomach and then slamming him to the ground was way over the top. But then what else could he expect from a mental case like Zane. He trudged off towards Blue's jail. Zane and the others began talking behind him in muffled voices. He struggled to hear. He heard the words ridge and plan, and then Richard distinctly said, "trouble," and Zane said, "Who cares?" What were they up to, he wondered.

He focused harder on listening, but they'd stopped talking. About a second later he found out anyway.

"What the . . . ?"

Zane and Richard threw him to the ground, took him by the ankles and began to drag him across the ground. Sticks and pine cones cut into his back. Two more defenders took hold of his arms and, laughing hysterically, they began to run with him. Charlie twisted and turned in vain to try to break free, even grabbing onto a bush, only to end up with a handful of painful thistles.

"Let me go, you idiots!" he screamed.

"Shut up, Apple Juice," Zane mocked.

Charlie suddenly realized they were headed away from the jail. "Where are we going?" he asked, getting a bit nervous.

"How would you like to take a trip to the ravine?"

Zane asked. He lowered his voice to sound menacing. "All together now, boys."

They began to swing him.

"Get lost. Let go. This is dumb," Charlie said, struggling to keep calm. There were rocks, bushes and scraggly trees leading to the ravine — and it looked a bit like a cliff. His heart was pounding. A feeling of panic spread up his back and a sick feeling filled his stomach.

"On the count of three!" Zane declared.

"One . . . two . . . two and a half . . . two and three-quarters . . ."

Charlie closed his eyes in relief. They weren't getting to three. Obviously they were only trying to scare him.

"Okay. Let's take A.J. to jail," Richard said.

"We totally got you, Apple Juice," another kid said, laughing.

The guys holding his arms let him go. His head banged the ground.

"You guys are chicken," Zane said. "I say no prisoners!"

He grabbed Charlie's right leg and pulled him violently towards the edge. Charlie grabbed frantically at a small rock lodged into the ground, just as Zane's foot thudded into his ribs. Charlie felt his grip slip away.

And then he was falling.

For the first five metres he slid sideways, but then his hip caught the root of a tree and he started somersaulting, bounding off tree trunks and skidding over rocks. Faster and faster he tumbled until he was dizzy and totally disoriented. A sharp pain shot down his arm when a branch jabbed into his shoulder. His hip crashed into a fallen tree, sending him right over and onto his back. Terrified, he closed his eyes and raised his arms to protect his head, as his back scraped along the corner of a rock.

And just when he thought it would never end, he thudded headlong into a large bush. It really hurt, and for a few moments he had to fight for his breath. But he wanted to give that bush a huge hug. Right behind it stood a massive boulder. He would have smashed right into it.

He could have been killed!

Charlie groaned and gingerly rolled himself out of the bush. At first he couldn't even get up and he just lay there on the ground. His entire body ached and he worried there might have been some serious damage. His hip was especially painful and his hands were bloody from grabbing the thistles, but, as he got to his feet slowly, he discovered to his utter amazement that, apart from some substantial bruises and scrapes, he was okay and hadn't actually broken anything. He could even walk without much trouble.

Although he had the scars to prove it, he couldn't quite believe what had happened. Zane had actually thrown him down a cliff. He really was psychotic. Charlie wanted to charge back up and pound him out. The only problem was he didn't have wings. It was way too steep. Hoping to find an easier section to climb, he followed a path that wound itself along the bank of the ravine. For what was probably about five minutes but felt like ages, he had no luck — until, suddenly, he spied a narrow channel leading up the side of the hill, which he figured was made from the spring runoff of water from the field. It was still a very sharp incline, but, he thought, the sides of the channel should give him a foothold, and there were also a few shrubs on both sides to grab on to.

"Come on, Apple Juice," he said to himself. "Time to climb."

The first stretch was fairly easy. Then it got steep and soon he was forced to climb on his hands and knees, the rocks and tree roots adding to the bruises on his body. His hip was really throbbing now. He pushed the pain from his mind. What other choice did he have if he wanted to get back in the game? Using the shrubs as handgrips, Charlie managed to struggle his way over what he thought were the worst parts. Then he arrived to about five metres from the top. Charlie's heart sank. Dead end.

No way was he going to be able to do that. He'd thought the climb to here was steep, but this was totally vertical. He scanned the surroundings for other options. About one-and-a-half metres to his right he noticed a thick tree root that jutted away from the side of the hill, forming a semicircle. If he could grab onto that root, maybe he could scramble up the side of the tree to the top. The only problem was, he'd have to jump for it — and if he missed, he'd almost certainly tumble right back down. He rubbed his hip and ribs. Not a pleasant possibility.

Climbing back down wasn't an appealing option

either, though, and if he tried another route, he'd probably end up in the same predicament somewhere else. Charlie took a minute to steady his nerves, closing his eyes and breathing deeply. Then, he opened his eyes wide and launched himself full out at the tree root. He caught hold and curled his fingers around it, but they didn't make it all the way, and he felt his hands start to slip. He bore his toes into the side of the hill, desperate for leverage.

He was going to fall!

Just as he began to slip, his right shoe hit something. Was it a rock? Charlie pressed into it firmly with his foot. It held! By pushing off from the rock, he was able to reach back up, wrap an arm around the tree root and pull himself up. The root scraped his stomach and ribs as he did, but he couldn't have cared less, he was so focused on reaching the top. Feeling around blindly overhead, he managed to get hold of a sturdy branch. "It's up and over time, Joyce," he whispered.

On the count of three, using the branch like a rope, he was able to hoist himself over the crest. Charlie immediately dropped to the level ground and lay on his back, battered, drenched in sweat and covered in mud and dirt, and replayed the entire incident in his mind.

The sound of muffled voices interrupted this restful moment.

"This is totally boring. We've been standing here the whole time. I want some action."

"Zane told us to guard the flag."

"Big deal. He ain't my boss."

"I wouldn't wanna mess with that dude."

"I hear ya. Guy's an animal."

"Dirtiest player I've ever played against. He butt-ended me yesterday in a stupid breakout drill, for no reason — just because."

"I can't believe what he did to that guy. What's his name?"

"Joyce. Charlie Joyce."

"He must be in some serious pain."

"I bet he broke some bones for sure — I mean, it's like a sheer cliff, no joke."

"He's that guy who messed with the rope on the obstacle course, right?

"Yeah; and I heard he lost his equipment and Jen went nuts on him."

"Zane's gonna get it, though; and maybe us too." It was Richard, and he sounded worried. "I don't really know the guy, but . . . well . . . that was crazed. He could've killed him."

"We didn't do it. Zane did. He'll probably get kicked outta camp."

"Like I care."

"I still don't see why we all gotta guard the flag the whole time. At least we should take shifts."

"I hear ya. I'm done guarding. I wanna take a run at Blue's flag, or at least tackle someone."

"Me too. Let Zane guard the flag."

"We can't all go," Richard said.

"As if anyone's gonna find it behind that tree. It's the best hiding spot of all time."

Three of the guys wandered away, with only Richard and one other hanging back.

Then all of a sudden it hit him. The flag! Behind a tree! Charlie looked up, and had to clamp his hand to his mouth to stop from laughing out loud. There it was, tied to the back of the bush — within arm's reach! They must have put it there thinking no one could possibly see it. He reached up and grabbed the flag.

This was the perfect time to act. Three of the guards had left, and the other two were a good ten meters away. Climbing down was obviously out. No option left but to outrun them. That wasn't the most appealing option either. He felt like his entire body was a bruise. His hip was killing, the thistles in his hands were really burning, and he had cuts and scrapes all over his arms and legs. But after what Zane had done, Charlie was ready to run through glass if it meant winning this stupid game.

He crawled as quietly as he could to the edge of the bush. Richard and the other kid still weren't paying too much attention to the flag. He got up, knotted the flag into a tight ball in case he needed to pass it, took a firm hold, and burst out from behind the cover.

"What the . . . ? The flag! He's got it."

"Red alert! Red alert! He's got the flag!"

"Get him!"

Charlie didn't look back. His only chance was to keep on going. He broke out of the forest and onto the field, sprinting up the sidelines, Richard and the other defender pounding after him. For a second he thought he was home free, until attackers from the Red team appeared in front of him and started to charge, Nick among them. To make matters worse, Jake and Markus were also stampeding after him from the opposite side.

Charlie was surrounded. He searched frantically for an escape.

"Charlie, I'm with ya!"

Slogger was tearing up field to his right. Charlie cut towards him.

"Take him down, boys."

Charlie waved Slogger off. "Go wide!" he yelled.

Slogger nodded.

Charlie ran right at Nick and his Red teammates. At the last second, he slowed and whipped the flag across his body to Slogger, and then threw his body forward, crashing into the would-be tacklers. Nick and two others were knocked clear off their feet, and the others had to jump to the side to get out of the way. As if he needed it, two guys ended up falling on him.

Had it worked? He would die if all this agony had been for nothing.

Thud.

Someone ran right into his ribs, and he gasped for breath.

"That's for being a loser, Apple Juice."

Charlie scrambled out from under the pile. Zane laughed at him.

Charlie took two steps forward and drove his forearm into Zane's chin, sending the bulky defenceman crashing to the ground. Before he could turn back around, however, someone else bodychecked him and he fell heavily on his hip, pain shooting up his entire side.

"How did that feel?" he heard.

Charlie looked up. Of course Jake would hit him from behind.

The next second, however, Jake joined him on the ground.

"Why don't you tell me how that felt?" Nick said. He reached down and pulled Charlie to his feet.

Jake and Zane stood up together. Zane's face was beet red. He was in a total rage. "You're done, Apple Juice. You're totally dead."

"I don't think so."

Slogger came up beside Nick and Charlie.

"Just try. We'll hammer all three of you," Zane snorted.

Simon shoved Jake aside and took his place next to Charlie. Gabriel joined next, and then Scott came tearing over.

"Bring it," Slogger said quietly.

Tweet. Tweet. Tweet.

"Gentlemen! Have you lost your minds? Fighting over capture the flag?" Jen was glaring at them with her hands on her hips.

Charlie kept his gaze firmly fixed on Zane.

"Get back to your respective teams, right now." She pointed at Charlie. "A word in private please, Mr. Joyce." Charlie stayed put, while the others rejoined their teams. "I'm really, really, really disappointed in you," Jen said quietly. "I think you're a good kid, and I've tried to be patient, but you have to admit you seem to be involved in . . ." She paused and brushed her hair from her eyes. "I mean, whenever I turn around you're in a . . . situation. I saw you attack Zane, and while I think Jake was out of line, and I'm going to talk to him about that right now, I don't understand your behaviour. Do you have anything to say?" As usual, she had no idea what had happened, or simply didn't care. Anyway, he didn't feel much like explaining.

"I'm tired of this bogus camp," he said fiercely. "I know you're not interested in the truth. All you're interested in is giving me a hard time."

Jen looked shocked. She gave her head a shake. "We'll discuss this later," she said finally. "Line up with your team."

As soon as Jen set off towards the Red team — presumably to speak to Jake — Nick and Scott came tearing over.

Charlie reached his fist out to Nick. "Thanks for bodychecking Jake out of the way."

Nick shrugged. "I should be thanking you for giving me the chance."

"You got to bodycheck Jake, and I missed it?" Scott slapped his forehead with his hand. "Tell me everything. Don't leave anything out, especially the part where Jake splats to the ground and starts crying like a baby."

"What did Jen say?" Nick asked.

Charlie shrugged. "She was on me about knocking Zane down."

"How could anyone be against that?" Scott said, throwing his hands in the air.

Nick suddenly grew serious. "Hey, Charlie. What happened to you? You're covered in dirt, and there's blood on your shirt, and —"

"Gentlemen, please go to your banners," Trevor ordered.

Nick and Scott gave Charlie a concerned look as he left for the Blue end.

Slogger met him halfway.

"Did you get across?" Charlie asked him. "What happened?"

Slogger opened his mouth to respond, then stopped and took a closer look at him. "Um . . . are you okay? You look all messed up. There's dirt all over your face, and your clothes are all torn. Hey, is that blood?"

Charlie could only imagine what he looked like. "I'll tell you about it later," he said. Zane, Richard and the others would expect him to tattle.

As he joined his Blue teammates, he saw Simon hold the Red flag over his head.

"Outstanding!" Charlie shouted, and he went over and gave Simon a high-five.

"It was a classic tic-tac-toe — a three-way passing play," Slogger explained. "You tossed it to me, I lateralled to Gabriel, and he flipped it Simon for the win."

"Wish I could've seen it," Charlie said ruefully, rubbing his sore hip.

"Where did you find the flag?" Slogger asked him. "We were looking all over the place."

"I heard you got captured," Gabriel said. "Who freed you?"

"I spotted the flag in a bush near the ridge," he explained. "Got in behind and high-stepped it up the field. Never would've made it without Slogger coming to my rescue."

The rest of the Blue team crowded around them.

Pete stepped to the front. "Awesome display. I only saw the last part when Joyce took out five guys."

"I don't think there were five," Charlie said modestly.

Pete turned to him. "You certainly paid the price. Can't believe you stayed in the game. How'd you ever get back to the field?"

"I saw the flag in a bush," Charlie said, hoping Pete wasn't talking about Zane.

Only that's exactly what he was talking about. "No, I mean after you got tossed. It's good to see you in one piece. That must have been painful."

"Slogger got the toss," Gabriel broke in. "Charlie threw the flag to Slogger, and then I got it and then —"

"Not the toss of the flag," Pete said. "I mean after Zane and his boys tossed Charlie down the escarpment. Some guys on the Red team told me. Wait till the coaches hear. They'll kick them outta camp for sure."

A murmur rose among the players and all eyes turned to Charlie. He swallowed hard. It was tempting to let things run their course and see Zane get what he deserved. But . . .

"I'm gonna forget about it. I'll get mine back on the ice."

They were silent. A slow grin crossed Pete's face.

"So you got the flag by . . . ?"

"Climbing back up right behind the bush where they'd hidden the flag," Charlie finished.

There was a long pause in which no one said a word. Then, all at once, everyone started cheering Charlie and high-fiving and hugging each other. Slogger gave Charlie's back a pounding, which made him wince.

"Hold it down over there. Can everyone come to centre field, please?" Trevor held the cup over his head. When they got there he said, "We'll start another game soon. But first, how about we present the hardware to the Blue team."

He felt a bunch of hands push him from behind, and Charlie went forward to take the cup. He thought he saw Jen's face harden when he took it. This time he didn't care what she thought. He'd earned it. Charlie took the cup from Trevor's hands and held it aloft.

Jen's expression suddenly changed. "Charlie, what happened to your clothes?" she asked in a concerned tone. "And you're bleeding on your —"

"As if you care," he snapped.

Charlie continued to hold the cup over his head as he ran back to his teammates. He heard someone from the other team call out, "Got your sippy cup, Apple Juice?"

But there was no way he was going to let them ruin this for him.

He clamped an arm around Slogger's neck and called out, "Victory lap, boys. Let's go!" and despite the throbbing in his hip, his burning hands, and the other scrapes and bruises on his body, he led the Blue team around the field.

APOLOGY ACCEPTED

Bang! Bang! Bang!

"It's open."

Nick and Scott came into his room. Charlie lay in bed.

"Don't you trust me to get up?" Charlie said, peeking out from under the sheets.

"Trust Charlie Joyce to be on time for anything?" Scott said incredulously.

Charlie threw the covers off. He was fully dressed. "Got ya." He slid tentatively out of bed, still sore from his fall down the escarpment and Zane's kick in the ribs, his hands still stinging from where the thistles had dug in. He could use a day off and, to be honest, he wouldn't be that upset if he was suspended for yelling at Jen.

Corey came out of the shower.

"How was the run?" Charlie asked him.

"Awesome. I tell ya, Charlie, I definitely had a bug at the start of camp." He stopped short. "Hey, boys.

What's shaking?" He turned back to Charlie. "My dad was right. I had no energy. Now I'm feeling strong again, and can play my game and dominate. I met with Coach Clark." He pulled on a sweatshirt and sweatpants. "Coach said he'd give me another look for Team 1 on account of my illness. So I really gotta bring it. Dad says I gotta treat every practice like Game 7 of the Stanley Cup Finals."

Corey's phone rang and he reached over and answered.

"Yeah, Dad. Capture the flag was good. I didn't, no. But practice yesterday afternoon was awesome, and Coach Clark . . ." He went back into the bathroom.

"I've planned things perfectly this morning," Scott said to Charlie and Nick. "We go downstairs, stuff our faces with breakfast, wait till Jen tells us to hurry up and get ready for practice, then keep stuffing, then Trevor tells us to go, but we keep eating until we're about to be sick, only that doesn't stop us, until we finally explode."

"I'm surprised you're not running this camp," Nick said.

"No kidding," Scott replied.

Corey came back out. "You boys ready for the skills competition?" he asked. He plugged his phone into his charger. They looked back at him quizzically. Corey laughed. "Forgot you boys ain't veterans like me."

Charlie suppressed a groan. Corey reminded him that he'd been invited last year about four times a day.

"There are three events: shooting, stickhandling and

skating. First, each team has its own competition to choose the top three guys in each event. Then the twelve reps for each event meet in the finals. They use a real radar gun for the shooting. No big deal for me since I go to a shooting class every week. I cranked one over 80 miles an hour last time I went, so I'm solid — won it last year, and I've gotten way stronger. The best part is the speed race, four guys at a time, two laps. It's a total riot — tons of contact round the corners, believe me." He slapped Charlie's back. "It'll be a battle royal between us speedsters."

"Well, good luck," Charlie said.

Corey snorted. "No such thing as luck. My dad says the guys who work the hardest are the luckiest." Corey pulled on his shoes. "Did you guys hear about Duncan? He got sent down to Team 3. He lost his binder. Second time too. Some people just don't want it, I guess." He stood up. "I'll see you guys at the rink."

He crossed the room and was gone.

"The guy's like a human tornado," Scott said, in a bewildered tone.

"He's something else," Charlie said. He put on a sweatshirt. "Weird about Duncan. He's a Team 2 centre, I think. Losing his binder sounds like something I'd do."

"Weirder things have happened," Scott said.

"Like the rope at the obstacle course," Nick said. "That's still an unsolved mystery."

"Not for long," Scott declared. "I know how we can track down the guy who messed with the rope."

"How?" Nick asked excitedly.

"We just have to find the person who carries invisibility spray. Then we have our culprit."

Nick rolled his eyes. "When will I learn?"

Scott flicked his eyebrows up and down a few times. "It's gonna take a few more years, Nick. It's not your fault. You're just not really very smart."

Slogger popped his head around the door. "Time to rock and roll, boys."

Charlie followed his friends down the hall to the cafeteria. Obviously he had his doubts about an invisibility spray; besides, he was still sure that Nathan did it, even though lately he didn't seem to be hanging out with Jake much. Too bad about Duncan. It put him on edge, though. If Duncan got switched for doing that, Charlie Joyce was certainly skating on thin ice, especially after his dustup with Zane.

* * *

Charlie and Slogger were among the last to walk into the dressing room, so most of the guys were already getting dressed. Cries of "Hey, Slogger," and "Hi, Charlie," greeted them. Slogger was well-liked, and Charlie had a feeling that's why they included him. It felt good all the same. He and Slogger took their usual spots next to each other in the corner. He unzipped his bag and pulled out his hockey pants.

"Yo, Charlie," Gabriel said. "I forgot. Jen wants to speak to you."

The butterflies in his stomach fired up pretty quickly. Not that he should be surprised, just that he'd somehow managed to put it out of his mind. He could kiss the skills competition goodbye, that was for sure. The room quieted as he left. They knew it too. He spotted Jen by the vending machines.

"Hi, Jen," he said nervously.

She raised an eyebrow. "Yes, Mr. Joyce. What can I do for you?"

That caught him off guard. She'd asked to speak to him. Anyway, best get the apology over with, and then take his punishment. He cleared his throat, stalling for time as he struggled to come up with the right words.

"I'm . . . um . . . I wanted to, like . . . apologize for . . . you know . . . what I said to you on the field yesterday. I . . . um . . . maybe I — no, I mean, I did . . . get angry. But not at you — at the other guys." He cast his eyes down. "I thought they had . . . I thought they had . . ."

"What did you think?" Jen said gently.

Her tone startled him. It seemed almost friendly. He couldn't bring himself to tell her the whole story, however. "I didn't mean it," he blurted. "I'm sorry."

Jen clasped the clipboard to her chest. "I appreciate that, Charlie. I really do. I understand this camp can be stressful, and I don't think it's been easy on you in particular." She took a deep breath. "There have been some rumours that capture the flag got a bit rough. Do you know anything about that?"

He shook his head firmly. He solved his own problems; he wasn't about to squeal on Zane to get back at him.

Jen unfolded her arms. "Because you looked rather nicked up after the first game?"

Charlie shook his head again.

"Okay. No problem. Do you need anything else?"

Charlie could hardly believe that she was going to let him off the hook. He felt the knot in his stomach disappear. "No, that was it. When Gabriel told me you wanted to speak to me I knew what it was about."

A playful smile crossed her face.

"I never said I wanted to speak to you."

He stared at her.

She smiled again, both eyebrows arched, and lowered her clipboard to her side. "Perhaps your friend Gabriel got confused."

Charlie felt like an idiot. "Yeah. Maybe. I'll go ask. Thanks, Jen."

He spun on his heels and practically sprinted back to the dressing room. When he walked inside everyone began laughing. He stood, bewildered, in the centre of the room. Did they hear him apologize?

"How was your talk with Jen?" Simon managed, as he gasped for air.

Charlie hung his head. He'd totally fallen for the prank. Gabriel was laughing so hard he was lying on the bench, and soon Charlie was laughing harder than anyone, and he gave Gabriel a high-five. He noticed Jake, Zane and Markus in the other corner didn't join in.

"That was harsh," Charlie said. "I sounded like the lamest dude in the world. She thought I'd lost my brain." He sat back down. "Were you in on that?" he said to Slogger.

"Not really — other than the fact that it was his idea," Gabriel said.

"You know this means war," Charlie said.

Trevor came in. "Hustle up, boys. Ice is ready and this should be a lot of fun. We'll warm up a bit, and then start the skills."

Charlie pulled on his equipment as fast as he could. Because of his talk with Jen he was last out — as usual, it felt like. He grabbed his stick, and was about to leave when the door opened and Richard came in. He had his helmet off, and he looked really nervous. A second later, two other players came in — Nathan, and a kid he knew by name only, James. They all sort of shuffled their feet, and mostly looked at the floor. The butterflies in Charlie's stomach went into overdrive. He couldn't believe they'd try anything in the dressing room, with coaches around . . ."

"Hi," Richard said.

"Hi," Charlie replied warily. None of them said anything. "You guys looking for something?" Charlie asked.

"Looking for . . . ?" Richard said, as if the question surprised him. "No. I'm not looking . . . I mean . . . we aren't . . . Actually, we kinda wanted to talk to you."

Charlie's mind raced. He didn't know if these three guys were friends. James and Nathan were on Team 2, so maybe they were buds. Richard was on Team 1, though. Besides, he'd given Richard a wide berth since he blew him off at the obstacle course, not to mention the capture the flag game.

"Talk about . . . what?" Charlie said, still feeling uneasy.

The three boys looked at each other and then back at Charlie. James flexed his stick. Nathan bounced his on the rubber flooring.

"We all feel bad about what happened at the capture the flag game," Richard said.

"We were jerks," James said.

"And we never thought Zane was gonna do . . . what he did," Nathan said.

"Zane said we were gonna just fool around and scare you," Richard said.

It dawned on Charlie that these were the three guys who dragged him to the ridge and swung him by the arms and legs with Zane. But they had let him go, and Zane had been the one to actually throw him over.

"I couldn't believe what Zane did. I mean — that was a whole lotta wrong." Richard lowered his gaze. "I just wanted to . . . like . . . apologize for that. We shouldn't have gone along with Zane, and stuff like that ain't what I'm about. It was . . . well . . . I wanted to apologize; and also to say thanks for not telling Jen or the coaches . . . and stuff."

"Me too," Nathan said.

"And me," James echoed.

They all looked up at him at the same time. Talk about awkward — four guys staring at each other.

"It's cool," Charlie said finally. "It was Zane, not you guys. I know you were just fooling around." He grinned. "Besides, if he hadn't tossed me over I never would've had the chance to climb up the hill and capture your flag."

The tension in the room seemed to instantly disappear. Suddenly, they were four guys at a hockey camp, joking around.

"I loved how you decked Zane on the field," James said.

"He deserved worse than that," Nathan said.

"It was a nice sight seeing him eat some dirt. A lot of guys are giving you major props for doing it. That psycho thinks he owns the camp," Richard said.

A question popped into Charlie's head, and out it came. "Did any of you guys hear anything about the rope at the obstacle course? Not sure if you remember but my rope had been thrown over the wall and Jake and I . . . I think maybe Nathan had gone before, or something, and I was wondering . . ."

The other two boys looked at Nathan.

"I don't remember the rope not being there, if that's what you mean," Nathan said. "I was definitely behind J.C.; he might've been over the wall when I was climbing over it. I just don't remember much else."

"I haven't heard anything about it," Richard said.

"Me neither," James concurred.

The door opened and Trevor came in. He sighed and held his arms up.

"Any of you guys interested in playing hockey?"

"We were just going over our strategy for the skills competition," Charlie said.

"Why don't you do that on the ice," Trevor said.

"Sounds like a plan," Richard replied.

"Good luck, guys," Charlie said to Nathan and James as they headed to Team 2's rink.

They both ran back a few steps and held out their gloves. Charlie gave each glove a punch and they took off again. He walked slowly up the corridor to the ice, thinking about their apology. It was unexpected, and it was big of them. Maybe they sort of owed it to him because he'd kept it quiet, but he knew how hard it was for guys to say sorry sometimes — and Zane had been the only one who did anything really wrong. Nathan's answer to his question was unsettling, however. He'd been so sure Nathan had tossed his rope over the wall, and now he was pretty sure Nathan was telling the truth. He seemed like a good guy. The rope was the one mystery he thought he'd figured out. Now he was back at square one.

Absorbed in these thoughts, he was startled when a loud voice called out, "C-man, heads up!"

Slogger fired a puck to him. Charlie laughed at himself for being so preoccupied and took a few steps to gain control, stickhandled a bit and then slid it back to Slogger. He skated in on goal, and from ten feet out faked a backhand and dropped it between his legs. Charlie followed up and one-timed it into the top left corner.

"Goal!" Charlie declared.

"Assist!" Slogger yelled.

They slapped each other's shin pads. Before they had a chance for another rush, Trevor blew his whistle to start the skills competition.

16

ROUGH PATCH

Charlie tied his skate laces together and tossed them over his shoulder. He forced himself not to get too stoked about the skills competition finals. He'd made two events: stickhandling and skating. The race had been total mayhem, with him, Savard, Gabriel, Jake and Tan all within two metres of each other at the finish. Their race had been so fast that all of them had made the final except Tan. Now he had to go to the other rink to face the winners of the other teams. Slogger had come second in the hardest shot, behind Burnett, and was waiting for him at the door.

"Come on, superstar. It's starting in, like, ten minutes," Slogger said.

Charlie zipped his bag up, grabbed his stick and walked to the door. "Slogger, you're always holding me up," he said.

Slogger grunted in reply and followed him down the hall.

Trevor happened to be at the front doors and held

it open for them. "I understand I'm holding this for two finalists," he said.

Charlie blushed, but Slogger wasn't too embarrassed to speak.

"Charlie's in two, although he shoots like a wuss so I had to step in there."

Trevor laughed. "Remember that Gretzky didn't have the most powerful shot and he managed to score a few."

"Not sure that's good advice for the hardest shot competition, Trevor," Slogger said.

"I guess you're right. Pound the rubber, Slogger."

"Will do."

They made their way to the other rink in no time and headed to the dressing rooms.

"We're in room 2 or 3," Charlie said. "Any preference?"

"I've always liked even numbers," Slogger said.

Charlie pushed the door opened and instantly wished he'd opted for the other room. Jake and Zane were there, Jake for skating and Zane for shooting. Savard and Gabriel were to his right and he chose to sit next to them, but the second he sat down they both got up.

"Is it something I said?" Charlie joked.

"Not this time," Gabriel quipped. "The ice is ready. What took you so long?"

"I had to wait for Slogger," Charlie said.

Gabriel's eyes narrowed. "Do you expect me to believe that?"

"I might have been a bit slow getting my skates off," Charlie said guiltily.

From across the room, Jake called out, "Good luck out there, boys. Should be fun."

Charlie wasn't sure who Jake was talking too. It couldn't be him.

"Stickhandling is yours all the way, J.C.," Jake said.

Savard seemed uncertain what to say. "We'll see. Lots of competition."

"Good luck in the race," Jake continued, in a friendly tone.

Savard nodded.

"I'll try to get a second then," Jake said.

"Yeah. Sure. Good luck."

He opened the door for Gabriel and followed him out.

Jake leaned back against the wall, eyes half-closed, his lips closed tightly together. "And of course good luck to my good friend Charlie Joyce. Two finals! My, my, well done. I'm so proud of you."

Charlie started to tighten his skates.

"And a hearty good luck to you too, Slogger — the boy with the nifty nickname. Hey, Joyce, I hear your good buddies, Scotter and Nicholas, also made the finals — for Team 3, but still . . ." He shrugged.

Jake and Zane got up. "Delightful chatting with you both, as usual," Jake said. Zane smirked and followed Jake out the door.

As soon as it closed, Slogger said, "I don't know how you put up with him. I'd lose my temper so quick

. . . I'd probably have been kicked out of camp by day two."

Charlie finished tying up his skates. "I don't understand Jake," he said. "He's the classic bully, but he doesn't get anything out of it. He actually can be funny — you saw him — and at school he's sort of popular. Only he always seems to make sure most people don't like him, even when he has a chance to make friends — even with the girls at school. I just figure it's better to ignore him as much as I can. I can't compete with him on the jerk front."

"He's the best jerk around," Slogger agreed, standing up. "You ready to rumble?"

"Why not?"

He and Slogger had barely left the room when Charlie spotted Corey running down the hallway. He slowed to a walk and grinned awkwardly.

"I think there are lots of seats, Corey," Charlie joked. "No need to hurry. The arena seats something like five thousand people."

"I know. I'm going now, to watch I mean." His face was very pale, and he looked uncomfortable.

"How'd the skills go?" Charlie asked, and instantly wished he could take it back. Corey was in street clothes, which meant he hadn't qualified for any finals.

"Broke my stick warming up," he complained. "Had to use a piece of junk. The flex was way too high. Then during the race I caught a rut in the corner. This is the worst camp ever. I lost my concentration and choked in the stickhandling." He looked off in the distance. "I'll see you back in the room. Hope you do well." He pushed between them and walked down the hall.

"That dude is from another planet," Slogger said.

Charlie didn't respond. Slogger didn't know about Corey's relationship with his father. He bet Corey wasn't looking forward to the next phone call.

As soon as Charlie stepped onto the freshly flooded ice, Scott and Nick came racing over.

"Competition must be weak if you two made it," Charlie said.

"What event are you in?" Nick asked.

"Stickhandling and skating," Charlie answered. "Slogger's doing battle in the shooting competition."

"Shooting competition?" Scott said. "That's too bad. I'm in that too, so you have no chance."

"I will destroy you," Slogger said to Scott, sounding like a robot.

Scott shook his head and his face got all pouty. "I know guys on Team 1 get cranky if they lose. Should I just let you win?"

"I think that's a great idea," Slogger said.

They both laughed and slapped each other's pads.

"Let's warm up and scare the competition," Scott said to Slogger, and they went to retrieve some pucks from the net.

"Ready to stretch the legs?" Charlie said to Nick, and the two of them skated around the rink a few times before Trevor blew his whistle and called them all to centre.

"The order of events is as follows: stickhandling, shooting, and the speed race. For the first two events players go in team order, with Team 1 going first, Team 2 second, and so on. The speed race is two heats of six skaters, and then a final. Give me the stickhandlers down at the far end."

Jen and Trevor set up the pylons in a zigzag pattern. When they were done Trevor skated over.

"Team 1 is up. Who's going first?"

Savard, Gabriel and Charlie looked at each other. No one wanted to go first. It was always better to relax a bit at the beginning by watching. Finally Charlie volunteered. He slid a puck to Trevor and stepped forward.

"You know the drill. Same as before. Stickhandle between the eight pylons and shoot the puck into the net. Miss the net and the clock continues. Cool?"

Charlie nodded.

"On your marks . . . get set . . . go!"

Charlie pushed the puck ahead of him and carved around the first pylon at the top of the circle, puck on his backhand. He whirled towards the second and carved around that, puck on the forehand. He got into a rhythm, and by pylon six he felt great, even faster than he'd done it last time. He zoomed around seven and powered on to the last pylon.

A groan went up in the crowd, and none louder than Charlie's. The puck had stuck in a patch of wet ice that hadn't dried from the flood. Charlie had to backtrack and retrieve it. He fired it into the net to stop the clock, even though he knew it was over. The delay would kill him; he couldn't win now against guys like Savard and Gabriel.

He whacked the boards and sat back on the bench. Scott and Nick came over.

"Not sure if stopping the puck like that was a good idea, Joyce," Scott said.

"Leave the cheering up to me," Nick said. "You totally suck at it." He patted the back of Charlie's helmet. "That was bogus. You should get another try. You were the first one. The ice will be perfect when the other guys go."

Burnett was standing nearby. "I thought you had it going, Charlie. Tough break."

"Don't think I could take J.C. anyway," Charlie said. "This is his event."

In fact, Savard was flying along as they spoke, proving Charlie right. He avoided the spot that tripped Charlie up by going a touch wider, and then fired it into the net. Gabriel went next and narrowly missed matching Savard's time by a tenth of a second. No one else was close. Third place went to Pete, who really impressed Charlie with his agility.

The shooting competition was fun to watch, especially with Scott's antics, although after the stickhandling, Charlie was a little down. After every shot, the speed was posted on an electronic display. Each player got three shots. In the end, Burnett edged out Slogger for the win — and Scott came third. That cheered Charlie up; and he still had the race to redeem himself.

The racers crowded around Trevor.

"You've already done this with your teams, but I'll go over the rules once more to be clear. You start on the goal line. Twice around, but the finish line is centre, so it's a bit more than two laps. No pushing. No cutting off. Careful around the nets. Fastest three players go into the finals. I put all the names in a hat, and pulled them out at random for the heats. Line up in the order your name is called, first player closest to the boards.

"Give me Jake, J.C., Pete, Nick, Mathew and Charlie. The rest of you will go in Heat 2 — you can hang at centre and cheer. When I blow my whistle, the race is on."

Charlie assessed the competition quickly. He didn't know Mathew, a kid from Team 4. The others he knew were good — all powerful skaters. From the last race, he knew that once you got behind it was hard to pass guys, especially around the nets. He decided to get as close to the front as possible, and then hope for an opportunity to jump into first at the end.

Trevor held up his arm. "On your marks . . ." he said, "get set . . ." He raised the whistle to his lips.

Tweet!

Charlie exploded off the line, and took about ten short strides to get going. By the top of the circle he was at top speed and was practically flying when he crossed the red line. He was totally focused on being in front for the first turn. At the blue line he risked a quick glance to his right. Pete and Jake were a step behind, and maybe he had half a body length on Savard, but not much. Nick was just behind him too. This was perfect, he thought. As long as he was in front of Savard, even by an inch, he could turn tight around the net and they'd all have to slow down.

He could hear the others breathing hard. Charlie ducked his left shoulder and, with his skates lined up one behind the other, carved around the net. His inside shoulder glanced off the netting, but it didn't slow him down. The guys in the stands were making tons of noise, cheering the racers on, and that fired Charlie up as he powered back. He'd done it. He was in first!

Charlie knew his speedy opponents wouldn't be far behind, and he'd probably surprised them by going out so fast and aggressive. They might also think he'd get tired. Well, they were in for another surprise. This was going to be his race. Charlie carved around the net and began the last lap. Savard and Jake were only a step or two behind him, so he didn't dare slow down. He lengthened his stride and forced himself to ignore the burning sensation in his lungs. He'd gone out hard. The last half-lap was going to be a killer.

The guys watching were really going crazy now, and the Heat 2 players were pounding the ice with their sticks. Charlie focused on the skates cutting into the ice behind him as he geared up for the final turn. Savard was on his outside shoulder. Charlie figured he'd try to make a move now, given there was only one turn left. Charlie drifted a little to the outside to force Savard wide and then carved hard around the net. It worked. Savard had to move over. Then, out of nowhere Jake tried to sneak inside Charlie and Savard. He got by the post, but the angle was too sharp and his skates gave out and he crashed into Charlie, who, in turn, crashed into Savard.

All three players wiped out, with Savard getting the worst of it because he was closest to the boards. Charlie and Jake sandwiched him and then fell on top. Charlie heard the other three skaters whiz by.

"What was that?" Charlie heard Savard sputter. "Get off." He slapped Charlie in the facemask.

What? Jake had caused the pileup. Then another glove hit him in the small of the back.

"Joyce cheats again," Jake said, as he struggled to his feet. "Knows he's going to lose and trips me. Typical!"

Charlie threw his gloves under Jake's chin and knocked him backwards. "You're the one that smashed into me. I'm so tired of your garbage, it's not funny."

Jake two-handed Charlie in the chest and he fell over Savard's outstretched foot and tumbled to the ice.

"Get off me, already," Savard yelled.

"Yeah, get off the dude," Jake jeered. He held out his hand and pulled Savard to his feet. "That's the second time this guy has messed with you in a race. I'm sick of him."

Charlie jumped to his feet, and was about to charge Jake when Trevor intervened.

"Hold on, guys. I want to speak to Jen. She probably got a better view from the stands. It looked like someone was cut off and . . ."

It was too much for Charlie to take. How could he

say "someone," when it was so obvious that Jake had cut him off.

"It doesn't matter," Charlie said to Trevor through clenched teeth. "Disqualify me. I couldn't care less about this stupid race or this stupid camp. Forget all of you."

He pushed past Savard and skated towards the door leading to the dressing room. Catcalls and jeers fell from the stands, and Markus and Zane were dissing him as he left the ice. The race was the final straw. How could anyone not see what Jake did? And what was with Savard punching him in the face? He lost all respect for him as of that moment.

Slogger, Scott and Nick were at the boards. "Meet us outside," Scott called to him.

He nodded, but didn't stop to talk. He was done talking, done trying to impress the coaches, done trying to do anything. He was done period. He'd get these last two days over with and go home.

So much for the best summer of his life. How about the worst?

17

BLAME GAME

Charlie stomped into the dressing room. He pulled off a skate and tossed it into his bag. He felt like throwing it through the wall! Alarm clocks that didn't work, ropes that flew from one side of a wall to the other, hockey equipment that magically disappeared, getting tossed down the escarpment, useless Zambonis that left water on the ice, and now a disqualification for no reason! This camp was haunted or cursed — or maybe he was.

He'd barely gotten his other skate off when the door opened and Trevor walked in, followed by Savard, Jake, Burnett and Slogger.

Trevor looked deadly serious. "Charlie, I told you to wait for me to speak to Jen. Under the circumstances, I can understand why you were upset, but still."

Charlie didn't know what to say. Why wait to hear them disqualify him? Meanwhile, Jake slumped to the bench and began to rip off his laces. He looked furious.

"Like I said, I spoke with Jen and she saw the whole thing," Trevor said in a calm tone. "She told me that

Jake tried to take you on the inside on that turn and he ended up crashing into you, which knocked you into J.C. I'm sorry I missed it. I was joking around with the guys at centre. I guess I was keen to see the ending. Anyway, Nick won the race and Pete came in second. It wouldn't be right to make them race again, although for the record they both offered to. We spoke to the coaches and they decided that you and J.C. should move on to the finals. We'll just have am extra skater. I guess you should get your skates back on. You'll probably need them, unless you have some fancy running shoes."

Now Charlie felt embarrassed about storming off the ice. "Give me a sec . . . and I'll get back on the ice. I'm sorry I lost it. Dumb reaction."

Savard stepped around Trevor. "I'm the dumb one, and I'm the one who should apologize. Sorry about the punch," he said. "No excuse for that." He held out his glove, and Charlie, feeling self-conscious, gave it a tap.

The whole time Jake was making sure everyone knew how mad he was by throwing his equipment around. Finally, he took his entire bag and threw it into the middle of the room. "This is a bogus camp and that was a bogus decision," he said loudly. "Joyce cuts me off, knocks me over, and I get DQ'd. That's fair, Trevor. Real fair."

No one was listening. All eyes were on the floor. They were looking at Coach Miller's Stanley Cup ring, which had popped out of Jake's bag.

"It's like Joyce can do anything and no one ever says . . ." His voice trailed off and then he, too, became mesmerized by the ring. "Where'd that come from?" he asked in a daze.

"From your bag," Trevor answered, slowly emphasizing each word. "Can you explain that?"

Jake stared up at him. Charlie had never seen Jake look like that. He seemed scared, like a little kid. Despite all the terrible things Jake had done to him since he moved to Terrence Falls, at that moment Charlie actually felt sorry for him. It must be an awful thing to be caught stealing in front of so many people. But that vulnerable moment lasted only for a few seconds. Then Jake's face hardened, and he looked mean again.

"I can explain it. Joyce put it there. He was in the room all by himself and wanted to get me in trouble. He didn't know I'd be disqualified, and he wanted to get back in the race. And he certainly wants me out of camp to guarantee himself a spot in the Challenge Game."

Charlie couldn't talk. He just couldn't. The shock robbed him of his power of speech. He stood still, mouth open, staring back at Jake.

* * *

"Jake's full of it," Slogger said. "We caught him red-handed. Of course he'd point the finger at someone else."

"No worries, Charlie," Nick said. "Jake's doing a Jake. The coaches are too smart for that."

"Nick's right," Scott echoed, and then added, as if he couldn't help himself, "although I can't believe I just said that. But seriously, this is the lamest thing he's ever done. No one will listen to him."

"One thing after another," Charlie said passionately. "Clark ordered me back to my room. They asked me tons of questions about where I'd been the morning the ring was stolen, and Jen was going on about my missing equipment."

"You were with us after the obstacle course," Nick said.

"And then we had a snack," Scott said. "I remember that." He patted his stomach.

"Then we had to piggy-back Team 2," Slogger said. "I remember that." He hunched his shoulders and held his arms out behind him as if he was actually carrying someone on his back.

"Apparently, Miller likes to work out in the morning, before breakfast, and he went for a skate. He left his ring in the locker because we were going back there for practice." Charlie sighed and rolled his neck. "You didn't see how he looked at me. He thinks I planted the ring on Jake. I know it. Jen was beyond mad. Even Trevor was looking at me weird."

"He won't get away with this," Slogger said. "Jake's a snake. Knew it the first time I saw him. Only guy worse than him is Zane. They deserve each other."

"Jake's done for," Nick declared.

"This whole thing makes no sense. Why would Jake steal the ring? I know what he's like — boy do I know," he said, and his friends laughed, "but stealing a Stanley Cup ring? Not sure Jake's that kind of guy," Charlie said.

His friends continued to offer him encouragement,

and he pretended to agree that everything would be fine, but he knew better. His feud with Jake was no secret, and Charlie had been alone in the dressing room just before the ring was found. Planting the ring would have been the perfect way for him to get back at Jake. And Jake was a good talker. Charlie had a sinking feeling the coaches would listen.

He was totally cooked. Worse yet, what would his mom say? She'd spent all that money and Danielle had given up her drama camp — only to have him kicked out for stealing? If he could turn back time he'd tear that invitation up into tiny pieces.

If only!

DECISION TIME

Charlie said goodbye to his friends and returned to his room. The reality of his situation had sapped him of all his energy. Even though it was only eleven o'clock in the morning he could have gone right to sleep.

"Take a shower, Joyce, and maybe you can clean off that bad luck that follows you around," he said aloud to himself.

"Go ahead, I'll wait." Corey smiled and sat up. Charlie flushed. He hadn't noticed his roommate lying on his bed. "I saw what happened. I thought Jake cut you off. You definitely got ripped on that call. You should go to Clark or Miller and complain. That's what I'd do, and if you want me to back you, that's no problem."

He obviously didn't know about the ring. "Don't much care about the race. Bigger problems," he mumbled.

Corey shrugged. "What problems? Did the coaches change the teams around?"

Charlie stiffened. What was he talking about? "No," he snapped.

Corey opened his eyes wide. "I get it. The stress level is major-league high, what with the Challenge Game lineup being announced tonight. I figure I'm in a good spot. I had a great practice today. And the coaches don't really care about the skills competition. You don't win games stickhandling around pylons. You win by playing hard, being smart, hitting, forechecking and scoring."

After what he'd just been through, Corey was tough to listen to. He told him about the ring to stop him from talking about himself.

"Wow! Did you take it? I mean, really?"

"No!" Charlie said.

Corey held up his hands. "I believe you; I believe you. I didn't think you were that type. That's wack, though. The ring popped outta the bag in front of everyone? Crazy. I never trusted that . . . um . . . what's his name?"

Charlie wished he'd never heard it. "Jake Wilkenson," he answered mechanically.

"That's right — Jake. I've seen him play a bit. Another guy who shouldn't be on Team 1. I bet he won't make the Challenge Game. I think he's overrated, personally. He doesn't go hard to the net. Perimeter player. No intensity. Of course, he stole the ring, so he's gone from camp anyway."

Charlie furrowed his brows. He must have Jake confused with someone else. Jake was a lot of things, but not intense? Definitely not. "That's not Jake," he said.

"He's got black hair — a fairly big guy . . ."

"I know him," Corey replied. "If I hadn't gotten sick, no way he makes Team 1. Savard's not bad. Got some skill, and he can skate. But he's soft on the puck. Doesn't go into the corners and pay the price." He puffed out his chest. "I'd love to go up against him. Use my conditioning and strength to wear him down and then dominate with the cycling game down low. I got him figured out too. He's weak going to his left."

"I'm gonna take a shower," Charlie said tersely.

"Go for it," Corey said.

His roommate's high spirits bugged him. He could be a little more sympathetic.

Corey had other things on his mind, however. "Assuming Jake's kicked out for stealing, which is a safe bet, I think things are set at centre, with you, me, probably Savard . . . and maybe that James guy. He's not bad. Not in our league, but you gotta have four centres. Defence will be interesting. Zane's a lock 'cause of his size. I got him all figured out too. You make an inside move, and then take it wide. He can't move to his right. Doesn't do a quick crossover . . ."

Charlie tuned him out. The Challenge Game was the last thing he cared about.

"Your bud Nick could make it," Corey continued. "Nice shot. Good skater. I think you hang out with another guy, what's his name — Slogger? He's okay. Do you think he'll make it? Can't believe camp's almost over. I'm only hitting my peak now. Getting sick was like the worst luck, don't you think?"

Corey would not stop talking. He kept jabbering on about different players, and how he knew their secret weaknesses.

"You did great for your first camp," Corey said. "I bet you learned a lot, right?"

Charlie opened the bathroom door.

"You learned a lot, right?"

It would be rude not to answer. "Uh, yeah. Right. I learned lots."

"At least you didn't lose any more equipment," Corey said, laughing.

Charlie closed the door behind him and turned the shower on.

As he showered up, something about what Corey had said kept bugging him.

He repeated the words "lose any more equipment" over and over in his mind.

Did he mean when Charlie couldn't find his hockey bag, or was it something else?

A crazy thought popped into his head.

He had to speak to Trevor right away.

Charlie washed up as fast as he could, got dressed, and headed for the door.

"Charlie! Where're you going? Coach told us to stay put."

Charlie closed the door behind him.

Corey did have a point. The coaches would freak if they found out he was disobeying their orders. But he had no choice but to risk it. He could only hope no one saw him. He knew Trevor's room was on the first floor, and so he headed to the stairs.

"Charlie!"

He whirled around, his heart in his throat.

Nick stuck his head out of his room. "Are you crazy?"

"You scared me to death."

"I heard your door shut and figured you were just coming across to our room. You must really want to get sent home."

"I know this sounds nuts, but I gotta talk to Trevor."

"Did you hurt yourself? Can't it wait?"

"It's not that. It's . . . I promise to tell you everything after I speak to him."

Another door opened and Slogger stuck his head out. "What gives?"

"Charlie's decided now's the right time to talk to Trevor."

"Have you lost your mind?"

"I might have," Charlie whispered. "I'll be back in a sec."

"I can't let you go down alone — I'm coming," Slogger said.

"Me too," Nick said.

"Don't leave me here alone," Scott whimpered. "I get scared in the dark."

"It's still light out," Nick said.

"I get scared when it's not dark out too."

"Come on, guys," Charlie pleaded. "We can't all go. It's too risky."

"You've been a walking disaster since camp started." Slogger folded his arms across his chest. "Besides, you can't even find Trevor's room."

Charlie raised his eyebrows. "That's where you're wrong, my friend. He's on the first floor at this end of the hall."

Slogger thumbed over his shoulder. "He's at the other end. You're going the wrong way. Follow me."

The four of them tiptoed as quietly as possible to the stairs. Once they were in the stairway, they ran down the stairs two at a time, skidding to a halt at the door to the first floor. Charlie put his finger to his lips, and slowly pushed the door open.

"Coast is clear. Follow me."

Charlie took off, but before he took two steps a hand grabbed his shoulder out of nowhere. Caught already!

He turned around and let out a deep breath — Nick!

"Don't do that!" he hissed. "You really are gonna scare me to death."

"You're going the wrong way — as usual," Nick said.

"I knew that." Charlie turned, ran to the end of the hall and knocked on the door as quietly as he could. No answer. Please let him be here, he prayed, knocking a little louder. He felt like breaking the door down. Couldn't anything work out?

"I guess he's with the coaches," Slogger whispered.

The door swung open.

"Charlie? Boys?" Trevor's eyes narrowed. "I don't think this is the best time for a visit." He looked over their shoulders down the hall. "I just came from the cafeteria. I was told to come get Charlie in five minutes. They want to speak to you again. And weren't you all told to stay in your rooms?"

"I know. Sorry about this," Charlie said. "I just have to ask you a question. It's really important. Please. It'll only take a second."

Trevor hesitated. "Fine. Get in, all of you," he said.

The television was on, and a large pile of white towels littered the floor.

"We don't have TVs in our rooms," Scott said.

Trevor sighed. "Being an adult has its privileges. But I'm assuming that's not the reason you're ignoring Coach Clark's explicit instructions."

Charlie snapped to attention. "No. Sorry. I have a question. Do you remember when I lost my elbow pads back at the beginning of camp? I used hockey socks instead, and banged my right elbow on the boards and you gave me ice. You remember?"

"Yes, Charlie. I remember."

"Anyway, about the elbow pads, did you tell anyone, I mean, anyone at all? Did you tell another player, or even a coach, or maybe Jen?"

"No, Charlie. I did not discuss your elbow pads with anyone. Why would I?"

"No reason. I needed to know, that's all."

Trevor peered down at him. "Will you please tell me what's going on, Charlie?"

Charlie hesitated. He thought he could trust Trevor, but he needed a minute to sort things out first. "Can I ask you a favour? Please?"

Trevor smiled. "You can ask. Sure."

Charlie laughed awkwardly. That hadn't come out right. "Um . . . What I meant was, can you do me a favour and give me a few minutes to sort something out before you come and get me to speak to the coaches. I'd really appreciate it, and it would help a lot."

"I don't mind doing that, but why?" Trevor said.

"I just need the time," Charlie said earnestly.

Trevor held up his hands in mock surrender. "I guess I could use the extra time to fold these towels. I'll come by your room in ten minutes."

"How about Scott's room?" Charlie asked. He knew he was really pushing it here.

Trevor stared at him, and Charlie wondered if he was going to change his mind. "Okay, Charlie. Ten minutes in Scott's room."

Slogger led the way back.

"Listen up, guys," Charlie said the moment Scott closed the door to his room. "I've got a question for you to think about."

"Anchovies or onions?" Scott said.

"And pepperoni, ground beef and pineapple," Nick added.

"Come on, nobody really likes pineapple on pizza. It's only for colour," Scott said.

Normally, Charlie would have laughed. But this wasn't the time for jokes. He was running out of time.

"I'll get you a pizza with anything you want on it — I promise. First, I need some help about a killer decision I have to make."

"About what?" Slogger said.

Charlie took a deep breath. "So. Corey was in my room when I got back from the rink."

"That's totally insane," Scott said, "since he's your roommate."

Charlie furled his brow. "I'll give you that. But he was in a strange mood, like almost giggling, and he couldn't stop talking about the camp and the teams and other players."

"I can't imagine Corey acting strange . . ." Scott said to Nick, pretending to be perplexed.

"Well, more strange than usual. He said to me that with Jake gone he'll get promoted to Team 1 and that he's a shoo-in for the Challenge Game. I've never seen a guy more stoked. He was beyond hyper."

His friends went all quiet.

"So I'm about to take a shower, just to get away from him, when he says, 'You did good — and you haven't even lost any more equipment.'"

"What does that mean?" Scott asked.

Nick's expression grew serious. "I think I'm getting it now."

"Getting what?" Scott said.

"Everyone knows about my hockey bag ending up in the wrong rink. I didn't tell anyone about my elbow pads, though — mostly because it was stupid," Charlie explained. "Like I said to Trevor, I ended up wrapping my elbows with hockey socks, and naturally I banged one elbow and got a nasty bruise. Actually, I have Slogger to thank for that, courtesy of a hip check into the boards."

"Don't mention it," Slogger said.

"Anyway, Trevor told me to look in the lost and found, and the elbow pads were sitting right on top."

Each of his friends nodded.

"Now here's the thing," Charlie continued. "I never told Corey about losing my elbow pads, and as you heard, neither did Trevor."

"So how'd he know?" Scott said.

"'Cause he's the one who took them!" Nick exclaimed.

Scott looked surprised. "When did you get so smart?"

"I've been doing brain exercises; they must be working."

"There's more," Charlie said. "The equipment comment got me thinking. Almost every time someone's gotten into trouble, or something's gone wrong, Corey's been around. At the obstacle course, before the finals, I spoke to Corey. He was all bummed out because his team didn't win. He told me he was going to watch the race and I saw him walk off down the course before it started. He would've known that I was behind Savard."

"Then he was the guy that tossed your rope," Slogger said.

"Exactly. He waited for Savard and Nathan to finish.

And do you remember my stupid alarm clock not going off when we did our fitness tests? Corey had left the room already. He told me he went for a run. I bet he changed the time or turned the alarm off."

Charlie had to force himself to speak slowly. It all made sense now. "And what about Duncan? He got sent down to Team 3 because he lost his binder, and Corey knew about it before anyone. I bet he took it. Now that I think of it, at the fitness testing, Corey knocked me into Zane. I can't prove it, but I'm sure Corey was behind my equipment ending up in the other rink. I remember him running across the field while all the other guys were watching the piggy-backing. Finally, we get to another piece of serious evidence. Today after practice, Slogger and I saw Corey walking down the corridor when we were going on the ice. I don't know why it didn't register then, but what was he doing there when he hadn't made any finals? He should've been in the stands with the rest of the guys. Corey probably figured everyone was on the ice already. He wouldn't know that I was late getting over to the rink."

"And that's totally when he planted the ring in Jake's bag!" Nick practically screamed.

"Shh!" Charlie pleaded. "I don't want anyone else to hear this, at least not yet. But that's exactly what I think too."

"All right, so why'd he do that?" Scott said. "What's the point?"

"'Cause he wanted to be on Team 1 — and, most

of all, in the Challenge Game. He basically has to be, because his dad is crazed about hockey. He wants Corey to play Junior or get a scholarship to a university, and even make it to the NHL. He pays for extra power skating, shooting sessions, personal training. He calls Corey at least three times a day. I swear Corey's on the phone for an hour every night telling his dad about practices. He's under unbelievable pressure."

"So he's killing off the competition," Slogger said. "First he went after Charlie. When that didn't work he took out Duncan, which did work because Duncan got sent to Team 3. But he had to get rid of one more centre to make sure of it — so he planted the ring on Jake."

"The dude's not dumb. After Savard and Charlie, he's the next top forward on Team 2 now that Duncan's in the doghouse," Scott said.

"I can't believe Jake didn't steal the ring," Nick said. "He finally gets what's coming to him, and he turns out to be innocent."

"What are you thinking, Charlie?" Slogger asked.

He'd sort of made up his mind the second he'd figured out the truth, and after talking it out, he was sure. Charlie wished he'd never met Jake, and he certainly wouldn't miss the guy if he got sent home. But he couldn't let Jake be blamed for something he didn't do, not when it was so serious.

"Well, I think I'm going to have to tell the coaches what I know," he said.

"Charlie Joyce saves Jake Wilkenson — sounds too bizarre for words," Scott said.

"Not to mention Jake accused Charlie of stealing the ring," Nick said.

"He turned on Charlie at the obstacle course," Slogger said.

"And hit you from behind at the capture-the-flag game," Nick added.

"Let's not forget the piggy-backing," Scott said.

"I'd prefer to forget that," Charlie said.

"Jake wouldn't come to your rescue," Slogger said quietly.

"Maybe that's the real point. I'm no Jake Wilkenson. Jake didn't steal the ring. I'd love to see him go — but not like this."

"I guess that means your roommate's gonna miss the Challenge Cup," Nick said.

"That's another reason I wanted to talk to you guys. I'm cool about telling the coaches that Jake's innocent. I'm very uncool about telling them about Corey."

"I understand you, sort of, about Jake," Scott said, "even though the guy is a total jerk and would never do this for you. But look at what Corey did. He framed someone for theft — and tried to get you booted off Team 1."

"I know it's weird. But for some reason I still can't blame him for what he did. I'm obviously mad about it; I could've done without looking like such a doofus with Jen and in front of the other players." He shrugged. "I can't explain it. Only, I would feel worse about getting Corey kicked out than if it was me. His father puts him under so much pressure. Can you imagine what would happen if he went home for stealing the ring? As crazy as it sounds, I still think of Corey as a friend. Deep down I know he's a good guy, even though he drives me nuts half the time."

"Only half the time?" Scott said.

"You're right," Charlie said. "It might get up to the seventy-five percent level. The point is . . ." He sighed heavily. "Hockey is a full-time job for Corey — even though he's our age."

"I think you might have made your decision," Slogger said.

Charlie grinned. "I guess you're right."

"I understand helping a friend," Nick said, "but are you sure about this? Think about what the coaches are going to say. They might accept your story about Jake — but what happens when you refuse to tell them about Corey? They're gonna be seriously unhappy with you. I mean, what if they send you home for not telling?"

"What can I do? Dude's my roommate."

They all laughed.

"If you're cool with it, then I'm with ya," Slogger said.

"Me too," Nick said.

Scott stood up. "While I hate to pass up a chance to humiliate Jake, and I wouldn't mind not having to deal with Corey, I have to admit that Joyce might actually be right here. Why can't doing the right thing mean you get everything you want and people adore you and you become unbelievably popular?"

"Thanks guys," Charlie said. "This helped."

There was a knock at the door, and Charlie's heart almost skipped a beat.

"I forgot about Trevor," he said. "And thanks for keeping this Corey thing quiet."

Nick leaned back. "Keeping what quiet?"

"Already forgotten," Slogger said.

"Done," Scott said.

Charlie punched fists with each of his friends. "I owe you one."

"As I recall, you owe us a pizza," Scott said.

"Consider it ordered," he said, as he opened the door.

19

OUT ON A LIMB

Trevor ushered Charlie into the cafeteria. The coaches were sitting on chairs, all in a row, with Jen standing off to the side. Charlie fought the tightening in the pit of his stomach. He needed to keep calm. Everything depended on him convincing the coaches that Jake didn't steal the ring without giving away so much that they figured out Corey did it, and if that meant him getting sent home . . .

"We have a few more questions," Clark said. "Please take a seat."

He indicated for Charlie to sit next to Jake, who promptly moved to the far edge of the bench.

"Jake, I think we've covered everything for the time being," Clark said. "You can go back to your room."

Jake got up, eyed Charlie closely and, with a defiant expression, walked slowly out. The coaches waited until the door closed completely, and then Clark leaned forward and pointed his pen.

"Jake has made a serious allegation against you,

Charlie," he said. "We spoke at the rink, and now that you've had a bit of time to reflect, I'm going to ask you again: Did you take the ring?"

"I did not," Charlie answered.

"Jake told us he believes you planted the ring in his bag after the race when you were alone in the dressing room, and that your motivation was to get him kicked out of camp." He paused and said, "I understand you and Jake are not exactly the best of friends."

"You could say that." Talk about the understatement of the year, he thought.

"Could you tell us again what you did the morning the ring was taken?" Clark continued. "I believe that was the day of the obstacle course, right, Jen?"

"Yes, Coach Clark," she confirmed.

Charlie took a deep breath and began. "I remember running to the cafeteria after the obstacle course for a snack. I was with Scott and Nick, and Slogger too. After we ate, Jen announced that changes to the teams were posted the bulletin board. I'm not sure if all of you know that we had a race at the obstacle course, and . . . well . . . Team 1 lost to Team 2, and Jen announced that Team 1 had to piggy-back the Team 2 guys across the field. I guess it was a reward . . . or like a prize for winning . . ." He avoided looking at Jen or Trevor. "I piggy-backed Jake, and then went to the rink to get ready for practice. That's when I saw Jen in the lobby looking for the ring. At least, that's when I found out Coach Miller's ring had been stolen. Of course, that's also when I couldn't find my hockey bag."

"Is that your recollection, Jen?" Miller asked.

She nodded. "I distinctly remember Charlie . . . and I think Slogger . . . being there together. I was beside myself looking for your ring."

"And after that she helped me find my equipment. Trevor did too," Charlie added.

"That's correct," Jen said. "We eventually found Charlie's equipment in the other rink."

"Well, let's put aside the mystery of Charlie's equipment for the time being," Clark said. "I remember watching the piggy-backing with Coach Miller and Coach Binns. How come you ended up carrying Jake?"

"He asked me. Jen said Team 2 guys could choose who they wanted."

"I don't believe I said that a Team 2 player could order you to carry him," Jen said.

Charlie turned to her. "I guess you're right. He just came over and said he expected me to piggy-back him, and I just assumed I had to."

Coach Clark's eyes narrowed. For a few moments he seemed lost in thought, and then he said, "I'm not seeing when Charlie would have had a chance to take the ring. But then, I also don't see when Jake could have done it. They were clearly both at the cafeteria when snack was over because Charlie gave Jake a piggy-back. The only chance they had would have been after the snack and before Jen made her announcement. That doesn't sound like much time, and somehow I doubt whether we'll find any witnesses who could remember if Charlie or Jake remained in the cafeteria the entire time."

"I also have my doubts that Charlie and Jake worked together to steal the ring," Coach Binns said.

The room grew silent as everyone reflected on the coaches' speculations.

Charlie gathered his courage. "I think I know who took the ring," he offered.

That got their attention.

"Go on," Clark said.

"The first thing, and the most important thing, is that Jake didn't do it — and neither did I."

Jen and Trevor took a few steps closer to the other coaches, so it felt like all of them were crowding around him. It wasn't a very comfortable feeling.

"You already told us you didn't do it. But how can you be so sure about Jake?" Miller asked.

"It's weird how that happened, actually. I admit that I was alone in the dressing room before the ring was found in Jake's bag," Charlie said. "What you don't know is that I ran into another player in the hallway before the skills finals begin. He was already changed, and when I talked to him he was all nervous and acting strange. We were joking around a bit, and he made a comment about me losing my elbow pads. At the time I don't think he realized that he'd given himself away, or maybe he thought I'd never figure it out . . ."

His voice trailed off as he realized they were staring at him. This wasn't going well. No one knew about his elbow pads. He needed to explain things — and fast. Clark looked as if he was losing patience with him.

"Sorry. I should backtrack. My elbow pads were

missing from my bag before my first practice with Team 1. Only Trevor knew about that." Charlie looked over at him. "Isn't that right?"

Trevor nodded.

"And Trevor told me he didn't tell anyone about that."

Miller cleared his voice. "Sorry to interrupt, Charlie, but you've lost me with this elbow pad business. What does Trevor have to do with your elbow pads?"

"I just spoke to Trevor in his room and he told me . . ."

"You talked to Trevor about your elbow pads in his room . . . before you came here?" Clark asked, shaking his head. "I thought I told you to stay in your room."

Charlie flushed. "You did, only I needed to find out if Trevor told anyone . . . about the elbow pads, that is."

Clark rolled his neck and sighed. Charlie braced himself. "Continue," Clark said finally, in a quiet voice.

"When I was taking a shower in my room after the skills competition, it suddenly dawned on me. If Trevor didn't say anything to anyone about my elbow pads, and I didn't tell anyone, then the only other person who could know is the guy who took them. So the player I saw in the hall must have taken them from my bag. Anyway, I started to think about the obstacle course, and I remembered that this same player was walking away before the final race. At the time I didn't think anything of it. I assumed he wanted to see the race better. Now I think he must have been the one who threw my rope over the wall."

"Then that means the person you're talking about was on Team 3 or 4," Jen said to him.

Charlie gulped and tried to slow down his thinking. That was his first huge mistake. He was letting them narrow down the list of suspects. Nothing he could do but press on now, however. "Then it all came together at once. For instance, this person had told me about Duncan's lost binder before anyone else. How come he knew? The only thing I can figure is he was the guy who did it."

Coach Clark help up his hand. "Charlie, I'm still not following your point. And while I'm intrigued as to why you would defend Jake considering what we know about you two, it still doesn't explain how the ring ended up in Jake's bag."

"Right. Good point. Well, the thing is I know who put Coach Miller's ring in Jake's bag, because he's the same kid who took my elbow pads out of my bag, and most importantly, the same guy who was outside the dressing room before the skills competition. I was the last guy out of the room, so that's got to be when he planted the ring.

"It's no secret Jake and I aren't friends. I guess we're kind of the complete opposite. But Jake wouldn't do it. He's . . . not that kind of guy — I mean, the type to steal a Stanley Cup ring. I was there and he was as surprised as anyone when the ring fell out of his bag. And if he did take it, why would he be so dumb as to put it there in the first place?"

"We have considered those points as well," Clark

said. "But aren't you forgetting something?"

Charlie shook his head. What did he mean?

"Who do you believe stole the ring?"

Charlie took a deep breath. "That's the problem. I can't tell you his name. I can tell you he did it for personal reasons that didn't have much to do with hockey." That was probably pushing it a bit, but it wasn't exactly a lie. It had more to do with Corey's dad than anything. "And I can promise you he won't cause any more trouble. But if I tell you any more you'll figure out who it is, and . . . I don't want this person to get in trouble. He has enough problems as it is . . . and, since you found the ring, and since I know Jake didn't steal it, and I didn't, I was really hoping . . . we could just forget about it."

Charlie finished in a rush. He suddenly realized he'd been speaking practically non-stop this entire time. Clark had a funny expression on his face, which made him nervous. Would they connect the fact that Jake, Duncan and he were centres? Would that lead them to suspect Corey?

Clark opened his eyes wide and looked at Charlie for an uncomfortable moment. "I think you should go back to your room while we discuss this."

Miller motioned toward the door. Charlie felt he needed to say something more before he left. "This has been an amazing camp, and I've learned a lot about hockey. I'm sorry I can't tell you who stole the ring; and I understand that you won't be happy with that. I'm . . . just sorry, but I can't tell you."

Clark raised his eyebrows and sat back in his chair. "Thank you, Charlie," he said quietly.

Charlie hesitated, expecting him to continue, but he remained silent. Charlie nodded at the coaches and left the cafeteria, and then sprinted up the stairs and opened the door to Scott and Slogger's room. In answer to their inquiring looks, he said, "No way to tell what they'll do. I think they believe me about Jake. I'm not so sure about me and Corey. Anyway, they told me that I should go back to my room, so . . ."

"Catch you later," they chorused.

Corey was doing push-ups when Charlie walked in. He hopped to his feet. "Where did you go? You were gone for close to an hour." He looked worried.

Charlie shrugged. "The coaches wanted to speak to me again . . . about the ring."

"Is Jake getting sent home? They aren't blaming you, are they?"

Corey's eagerness to have Jake kicked out bothered him. "I don't think Jake stole it. Do you?" Charlie asked.

Corey shuddered ever so slightly and he began to blink rapidly. "The ring was in his bag," Corey said. "I don't see how he can deny it." He pointed to the floor. "Do you mind if I pump out a few more push-ups, and then finish with my sit-ups?"

Before he could answer, Corey was back at it. Charlie left him alone — he couldn't exactly talk to him while he was grunting and sweating — and lay down on his bed. Corey counted up to fifty push-ups, and then moved on to the sit-ups.

Charlie wondered what kind of dad made his son that obsessed with hockey, or with anything for that matter? He folded his hands behind his head and thought about his own father. Sometimes parents would get carried away at games and start yelling at the refs or other players. His dad would always ask them to be quiet. He used to get so embarrassed, and his teammates would bug him about it. Now he found it hard to believe he ever felt like that. He could see why it bothered his dad so much. Parents got so crazy about hockey and wrecked it for everyone. Corey was the perfect example. All those phone calls from his dad, and the extreme things he'd done just to get into the Challenge Game; he was so intense and under so much pressure that Charlie doubted he was having a very good time at hockey camp — and he'd ruined it for him, Jake and Duncan, just to try to live up to his dad's ridiculous expectations.

Corey kept up the sit-ups, pushing himself to do more. Charlie didn't feel like confronting him now. He tried to relax, but with little success.

How could he, with the coaches in the cafeteria right now deciding his fate?

UNITED FRONT

Charlie practically leapt out of his bed when he heard a knock on the door.

"Down to the cafeteria," a voice ordered.

It sounded like Trevor.

"We didn't have a meeting scheduled, did we?" Corey said. "I need a shower."

"I think it's a surprise," Charlie said dryly. Corey hadn't stopped exercising the entire time. Charlie was almost thankful that the moment of truth had come.

Slogger was already in the hallway.

"Did you know about this meeting?" Corey asked.

"It's a surprise, I think," Slogger said.

"Hey, that's what Charlie said." Corey laughed and slapped Charlie on the back.

Slogger gave Charlie a quizzical look, as they headed down to the cafeteria.

Scott and Nick were walking down the hall.

"You fellas know what this meeting is all about?" Corey asked.

Would his friends resist the temptation?

Nick whispered something in Scott's ear.

"Might be an award for the best-dressed defenceman — obviously me," Scott said.

The joke was weak and Scott knew it. But he stayed true to his word, and that was the end of it. Charlie relaxed. His friends would keep the secret. In short order, all the players had taken their places in the cafeteria.

Jen clapped her hands a few times. "Gentlemen. Let's settle down, please." She waited for silence. "We've decided to announce the lineups for the Challenge Game now instead of after dinner. Before we do that, Coach Clark wants to talk to you."

Coach Clark seemed more serious than usual. He cast his eyes around the room, settling them briefly on Charlie.

"As all of you are well aware, a few days ago someone took Coach Miller's Stanley Cup ring. This is easily the most unpleasant thing that's happened in the twenty years we've run this camp. To say the theft showed a lack of respect for the YEHS, Coach Miller and the game of hockey is an understatement. As well, the ring is worth a great deal of money, and stealing it is a criminal offence. The police were called and were beginning to investigate. This afternoon the ring was found in Jake's hockey bag. He denied taking it, and accused Charlie of putting it there.

"About half an hour ago Charlie addressed the coaches, and he stated to us that he did not take the ring, and that he did not believe Jake took it either."

A murmur rose among the players.

"Charlie also stated that he knew who took the ring, but that he wouldn't tell us who did it. When we pressed him for a name, Charlie said that he didn't want this individual to be punished, and promised there wouldn't be any more trouble."

Charlie couldn't help glancing over at Corey. He'd gone completely pale, his hands gripping the bottom of his seat.

"I should clarify for the record that Charlie cannot prove absolutely that Jake didn't take the ring. His evidence is based on certain suspicious behaviour and comments made by the unidentified thief. It is not the strongest evidence, but at the same time I cannot entirely dismiss it. There is also the plain fact that Charlie is so insistent that Jake did not steal the ring.

"As my dad used to say, this puts us firmly on the horns of a dilemma, which is another way of saying we don't know exactly what to do. I think the coaches all agree that Charlie is being sincere and truly believes Jake is innocent. On the other hand, he's covering up a crime."

Clark took a few steps forward and his face took on an even more serious expression. Charlie's chest tightened.

"The coaches have decided that in light of the circumstances, and after speaking to Jake and Charlie, we no longer consider Jake a suspect. He will remain in camp and is eligible for the Challenge Game. As for

Charlie, while I respect his desire to protect a friend, and admire his willingness to prove Jake's innocence, his refusal to identify the real thief cannot be condoned or ignored. There is only one day left in camp, and we do not see it necessary to send him home. Charlie is not eligible to play in the Challenge Game, however."

An eerie silence followed. It was a bizarre moment for Charlie. Corey was only about ten seats away. He was sitting ramrod straight, his hands clenched together in his lap, barely moving a muscle. He looked ready to break into a thousand pieces. Seeing Corey like that convinced Charlie that he'd made the right decision. It would absolutely destroy his roommate to be caught. Charlie couldn't do it to him, and if it meant missing the Challenge Game, then that was a price he was willing to pay.

Charlie slumped in his seat. They'd probably start to announce the lineups for the Challenge Game now. He wondered if Jake would make it.

"I don't think that's really fair, Coach Clark," he heard someone at the far end of the cafeteria say.

Charlie looked around. Richard was standing up and had walked towards the middle of the aisle.

"Coach Miller has his ring, and I don't think Charlie should be punished for telling the truth. He didn't have to help Jake," Richard said with real emotion.

Clark seemed taken aback. "The coaches have made their decision, but I understand your position."

"I think it's unfair too." Gabriel stood up, not far

from Charlie. "Is it really that important to find the thief if Charlie says the guy won't steal again? Charlie probably knows the guy well enough to say that, and I trust that if Charlie says the guy won't be a problem, then he won't."

Simon stood up next to his friend. "I agree. Charlie should be allowed to play."

"I wouldn't feel right about the Challenge Game if Charlie loses a spot because of this," Slogger said next.

Charlie fought to control his emotions. He'd never thought that these guys would be such true friends.

"We want Joyce! We want Joyce!" Scott and Nick began chanting and then all the players began talking at once. Coach Clark held up his hands. "Hold it down, boys. Hold it down. Again, I appreciate your willingness to help a friend, but . . ."

J.C. Savard stepped forward. The players quieted down. Charlie was totally surprised. While Savard was possibly the best player at camp, which gave him a lot of status, he wasn't that vocal and he rarely spoke in groups. Was he going to support him too?

"I wish you would reconsider, Coach Clark," he said. "I don't think any of the guys would feel right about Charlie being banned from the Challenge Game. I've played against him, and at this camp I've played with him, and I think he deserves the chance to play."

His buddy Burnett spoke next. "I'm with J.C. on this. I think he should be eligible."

A half-smile played across Clark's face. His head tilted to one side, he closed his eyes slightly and nodded a few times. "Before another ten of you ask, I will discuss this with the other coaches. Give me a minute, please."

Clark huddled with the coaches, and Jen and Trevor joined them too.

Nick and Scott gathered around Charlie.

"I thought you should've been tossed out of camp, but I didn't want to say it because we're friends," Scott said.

"That's a weird coincidence, because I wanted Scott kicked out," Nick said.

Charlie was grateful for their attempt to lighten the mood, and he laughed. Savard, Burnett, Gabriel and Simon came over.

"Thanks for the support, guys," Charlie said, feeling a bit awkward about the whole thing.

"You deserve to play," Simon said emphatically.

Slogger, Pete, Richard, Nathan, James and a few other guys from Teams 1 and 2 joined them too, and soon they were all joking around, Scott and Nick leading the way, naturally. Charlie did notice another smaller group of guys had formed around Jake and Zane. He could guess what they were talking about.

Things got fairly loud as time passed and at first no one heard Clark trying to speak. A piercing whistle interrupted their conversations.

"Thanks, Jen. I wish I knew how to do that," Clark said, laughing. "And now, gentlemen, would you please take your seats."

They laughed politely and sat down.

"We had an interesting discussion to be sure," he

said. "One thing I am emphatic about is not being afraid to change my mind. Sometimes I think referees refuse to reconsider a call because they fear that will lead to players or coaches questioning every call they make. I see their point, but a bad call is a bad call.

"In that spirit, we have decided that after hearing the opinions of the players who have had the courage to speak out in Charlie's defence, and considering their objections to our decision, I am prepared to reinstate Charlie for the Challenge Game."

The players around Charlie clapped and cheered, and Scott and Nick and a bunch of others gave him a high-five.

Clark held his hands up again, and they settled down. "With that bit of unpleasantness behind us, we can move on to more important matters — namely, announcing the lineup." Jen handed Clark a clipboard. "When your name is called, come up beside me, please."

He started calling out names. Jake's name was called, which got a reaction. His friends cheered, but Charlie noticed a few guys shaking their heads. Nick got called, and Charlie hooted and hollered along with Scott and Slogger. Then Slogger got the call, and Charlie flashed his new friend a big thumbs-up. Corey's name was announced, and his roommate threw his fist in the air. He looked ready to explode, he was so happy.

". . . and, last but not least, Charlie Joyce."

He felt Scott push him forward. Clark beckoned with his head for him to join the others. A rousing cheer sounded, and not just from his friends this time. He tried not to blush. He also didn't trust his legs, and was grateful when he found himself standing next to Slogger without having tripped over anything.

Clark raised an arm. "I give you your Challenge Game players. Let's give them a cheer for this accomplishment."

Coach Miller led everyone through three Hip, hip, hoorahs.

"Isn't this the coolest?" Slogger said.

Charlie had to agree.

FORMIDABLE FOE

Charlie circled the net and pushed hard to the blue line in an effort to slow the butterflies in his stomach. A quick meeting had followed the announcement of the Challenge Game rosters where Miller and Binns drafted the teams. Charlie ended up on Binns' team; and, intentionally or not, Miller took Jake. The next morning, his team met with Coach Binns to go over the lines and some basic strategy. He was stoked when Binns announced he'd be centring a line with Simon and Gabriel. Then the team was asked to come up with a name. After a few bogus suggestions, someone called out the Sharks, and no one objected. It turned out Miller's team wanted a dangerous name too and chose the Cobras, so it was going to be the Sharks versus the Cobras.

"Charlie, come here for a sec."

At the Sharks' bench, Binns and Corey waved. Charlie glided over and leaned an elbow against the top of the boards.

"We need a big game out of you two. I figure J.C. and Jake will generate most of the Cobras' offence. Both are excellent players, very fast, great shots, and instinctive scorers. Be aware of J.C.'s creativity with the puck. We can't afford to let him control the puck in our end. Get on him fast and try to keep the puck off his stick. As for Jake, he'll try to overpower you if he can. Focus on positioning, and keep your feet moving. He's a tough customer in close, so make sure you keep yourself between him and our net."

"Got it, Coach," Corey responded. "We'll shut them down, and pop in a couple too. This is when the hard work pays off. You can count on us."

"I like your confidence," Binns said.

Corey grinned and slapped Charlie on the back.

"So can my line start?" Corey said. "We're totally ready to get on the forecheck and bang some bodies. Do you mind, Charlie? Thanks, roomie," he said before Charlie could respond.

"Let's be sure to stay calm," Binns said.

It seemed to Charlie that Binns was speaking to Corey.

"I'll make adjustments as needed. Why don't you go finish your warm-ups."

"You got it," Corey answered for the both of them.

Charlie pushed off, looking for a puck to take a few shots on net. He'd barely moved when a stick slapped his shin pads.

"I've got mega-energy today," Corey said. "The batteries are totally charged. I'll be taking a little extra time on each shift to grind J.C. and Jake down. That'll make sure you're fresh." Corey tapped his shin pads again. "You'll do fine, Charlie. It's only natural to be nervous. I've been here before, and played in lots of big games. Leave the hard work to me."

He whacked Charlie's pads a third time and skated off.

The ref blew his whistle and the players skated to their benches.

"Let's have Corey's line out first," Binns announced. Charlie took a seat next to Simon and Gabriel to wait — and wait he did. True to his word, Corey stretched the shift and stayed out for almost two minutes. By the time Charlie finally got on, his linemates had come off and he had to shift up too.

It became obvious early on that Corey was having trouble keeping up with Savard. He was obviously fit, but the skill level made it a bit of a mismatch. On one play in the Sharks' end Savard slipped the puck between Corey's legs and then flung a saucer pass across the crease to a wide-open Cobras player. Only a helpful goalpost kept the puck out. The Cobras players changed up after that, as did Corey's wingers, and again, Corey stayed out as promised, leaving Charlie to cool his heels on the bench. Fortunately, the ref whistled the play down on an offside and Corey had to come off.

"Change up a little faster there, Corey," Binns called out.

Corey nodded to Charlie as he came off, but didn't say anything.

Charlie hunched over for the draw. Jake was a formidable centre, very strong and hard on the puck. He knew from experience that Jake often used his size and strength in the faceoff circle, not to mention the occasional cross-check. Surprisingly, the only thing Jake used his stick for was to try to draw the puck to his defence. Charlie was a hair quicker, however, and the puck went spinning back to the Sharks' left defenceman.

Charlie held Jake up slightly to give his defenceman time to move the puck, which he did by swinging it wide to his defence partner. Charlie cut deftly up the middle and promptly received a hard pass two feet past the blue line. An opposing winger challenged. Charlie saw it coming and cut inside to get the angle, then flipped it wide to a streaking Gabriel flying up the wing.

Simon came off the left side calling for a pass, and Gabriel didn't disappoint. Meanwhile, Charlie hightailed it to the far side vacated by Simon. It was a three-on-two, although Jake and his linemates were hustling back. They wouldn't have much time for a play.

Simon seemed to agree. A left-handed shot, Simon veered that way with the puck on his forehand, drawing both defencemen over. Charlie drove for the net, which forced the defenders to hesitate. That gave Gabriel the opportunity to get behind the defenceman on the right side. Simon whipped the puck across his body. Before the defenceman had a chance to react, the speedy winger was in alone.

Gabriel faked left, then right, dropping the goalie to his knees. He had an easy forehand up high, Charlie thought. Instead, he slid it across to Charlie. It was a totally unselfish play. Charlie banged the puck past the goalie's outstretched pad.

The players in the stands went wild, clapping and banging the back of their chairs.

"Great follow up," Simon said, slapping the top of his helmet.

Gabriel tapped each player on the mask. "Good hustle, boys. That was a sweet."

The Cobras changed forwards, and Corey hopped over the boards.

"What's with the quick shift?" Simon growled.

Charlie had only been out thirty seconds because of Corey's extra-long shift. He didn't see the point of complaining, however, and headed to the bench.

Savard won the draw back to the left defenceman, who one-timed it off the boards to his winger. He sent it spinning into the Sharks' zone as his linemates gave chase on the forecheck.

"You've barely had a chance to stretch your legs," Simon said to Charlie on the bench. "We pop one in and that clown comes bouncing over."

Gabriel spit some water over the boards. "I still think Duncan deserved the fourth centre spot. Corey's a solid player, don't get me wrong; and the guy's fit —"

"But he's got hands of stone," Simon cut in.

"He got invited last year —" Charlie began.

"I played in a tournament against him last season," Simon interrupted. "The guy was almost as big then as he is now. He used to overpower everyone. I say he's peaked, though. Now others are catching up in size. Like I said, he's got the hustle and the heart — but the skill's not there."

"Look at that," Gabriel interjected.

Savard had snagged a loose puck at the far boards. When Corey moved in to forecheck, the slick centre spun to his right and rolled around him. At the hash marks he let a slapshot go that caught the top left corner.

"Charlie, you gotta cover Savard," Gabriel stated bluntly. "Corey can't handle him. Coach doesn't make the move, we're done."

Binns patted the three linemates on the helmet. "We need that goal back. Get ready to change up."

He didn't necessarily disagree with Gabriel, but it was hardly his place to say that. He hopped the boards and skated to centre for the faceoff. Jake had already set up.

"Centreman, put your stick down, or I'll drop the puck," the ref barked.

That snapped him out of his fog. Too much time had been spent thinking about Corey. He'd done enough damage. Now the time had come to focus on Charlie Joyce.

PICTURE PERFECT

As the game continued, it became clear that Gabriel had been right. Savard and Jake were starting to get the better of Corey — in the faceoff circle, on the forecheck and in the Cobras' end. It was even becoming a bit of a joke on the bench, in whispers and cruel quips. Charlie thought Corey simply needed to relax. He was trying so hard that he was giving the puck away and making bad passes. At the end of the second period the score stood 3–2 for the Cobras. Gabriel had potted a wraparound for the second Sharks marker.

Binns called his team to huddle up. He didn't look too happy. "We seem to be having a hard time generating any pressure. We're lucky that it's still close — we can thank our goalie for that. Best we shake things up a touch. Charlie, I want to match you up with Savard. When he comes out, I want you and your line out there."

Corey stared hard at Charlie before taking a seat on the bench.

Savard was waiting for Charlie at centre.

"I had a feeling I was gonna see more of you this period," Savard said.

"I was waiting for you to slow down," Charlie joked.

The tireless star grinned and leaned over for the faceoff. The ref dropped the puck awkwardly and it skidded to one side. Charlie pounced on it, and Savard was right on him. Simon and his counterpart moved in also. A wild scrum developed, with the players in the stands screaming encouragement as they battled for puck possession.

Charlie was the one who managed to knock it free to his defenceman. Savard forced the defenceman to get rid of the puck wide right. Gabriel knocked the bouncing puck to the ice while pushing back against the Cobras left winger. Charlie gambled on Gabriel's puck skills and scooted up the boards. Gabriel didn't let him down. He swung around and fired a nifty carom off the wall and onto Charlie's stick.

He took the pass skating backwards, then spun around and weaved his way towards the blue line. A quick glance told him Savard was hustling back. For a second he was tempted to try to split the defence. But then he remembered Trevor's advice back at the beginning of camp: never turn the puck over in the neutral zone — get it deep! He hesitated with the puck, swerved a step to his left to give Simon and Gabriel a chance to build up speed, and then dumped it into the left corner. No way he'd give Savard a chance to counterattack on a turnover.

That's how it went for most of the third period. Each team settled into a rhythm and worked equally hard at both ends of the ice. Scoring chances were few and far between. Savard and Charlie battled each other to a standstill. Corey did a little better against Jake and for the most part held his own. Unfortunately, with about three minutes to play, Jake tapped in a rebound from close in to give the Cobras a two-goal cushion.

As the game wound down, Charlie had the puck near the wall at his own blue line. Gabriel hovered near the Sharks' bench, and Simon was stationary at the red line. With the lead, Savard held back so as not to get caught up ice. For practically the first time, he had some free ice ahead of him, and Charlie decided to take advantage.

He fired the puck to Simon and took off up the side. "Right back, Si," he yelled.

Simon led him perfectly and Charlie stormed over the red line.

"I'm with ya, Charlie."

That was strange. Sounded like Corey. Charlie did a double take. Corey had taken Gabriel's place. Corey would do what he always did — go hard outside and try to cut to the net. The defenceman would head him off and the play would be done. That decided it. Charlie faked the pass and drove between the two defenders. Before they sandwiched him Charlie slid a soft backhand around the right defenceman's skates, and with only his right hand on the stick jumped sideways to the outside. The defender stuck out his hip and Charlie barely avoided a punishing check, almost losing an edge. At the last second, he was able to regain his balance and find the puck.

The noise from the stands spurred him on. Forget the score, he thought. Time for his A-move. He'd been working on it in practice. Drop the puck to his right skate, and kick it back to his forehand. Suddenly, a voice called out to ruin the moment.

"Charlie. Over. I'm here."

Corey's stick smacked the ice.

"Use me. Use me."

He'd look like a hog if he didn't pass. Charlie took the puck to the outside post to sell it and when the goalie drifted over, he backhanded a pass to Corey. The goalie stuck out his left pad in desperation. The entire upper net was open. All Corey had to do was slow down and snap it home.

Instead, he one-timed it directly into the goalie's pads. Charlie had already raised his stick. Groaning, he returned dejectedly to the bench.

"What were you thinkin', Joyce?" Simon said with a smirk.

"May as well pass it into a black hole," Gabriel laughed.

Charlie took a sip of water. "Game's basically over. Doesn't matter."

"Not yet, it ain't," Gabriel said. "We should get one more shift. We gotta make it count. Time for one more goal."

"Time for two," Simon stated.

Charlie stifled a laugh. These two weren't joking. He drank some more water, and checked out the time. Two minutes left. Maybe there was time — if he could get Corey off.

Charlie rose to his feet. Burnett had beaten Corey to a puck at the blue line, and then, displaying his amazing athleticism, banked it off the wall and raced around the centreman to gather it up.

"Get ready, boys," Charlie said. He wanted those two minutes. "Corey, change 'em up. Come on."

Corey looked over, startled by the command. He shook his head. But Charlie's desire to play was overwhelming. He had to get out there, even at the risk of a too-many-men on the ice penalty.

"Corey, change up," Charlie bellowed, and he leapt onto the ice and joined the play.

Burnett had taken the puck deep into the Sharks' zone. Charlie raced towards the goal, hoping Corey had listened. The Cobras had two players in front, with the defenceman waving his stick trying desperately to cover both. Burnett recognized the mismatch and sent a hard pass to the player in the high slot. Charlie threw himself headlong, stick extended, and managed to nick the puck to the right boards.

The Cobras player grunted in surprise.

Charlie popped up on his left knee and stuck out his right skate to stop himself from sliding into the boards. "I've got the guy in the high slot," he yelled at his defenceman.

He nodded, and put a body on the other Cobras

forward and pushed him to the side. That gave Charlie time to assess the situation. The Cobras' left defenceman had hammered the puck down along the wall to Burnett. He had his back to a Sharks defender and was working his way towards the hash marks. Jake was stationed to the side of the net. They were going to cycle the puck and take time off. Both were skilled and powerful players. The Sharks might not get the puck back until it was too late.

The defenceman did a good job preventing Burnett from curling into the slot. That forced him back towards the boards. Jake moved in to begin the cycle. No sense watching, Charlie figured. The Cobras had probably won the game. He just wanted one more chance to score — for Simon's and Gabriel's sake as much as for his own.

He left his man in front and ducked in between Jake and Burnett, praying that the defenceman wouldn't anticipate his wild gamble — and it worked. Charlie intercepted the puck off the boards. He was in a difficult spot, though, sandwiched between Burnett and Jake, and no one breaking clear. The safe play would be to fire the puck off the glass and out. For the second time, he threw caution to the wind and cut sharply up the middle of the ice right beside the goalpost, banking on Burnett and Jake being tired after a long shift. He heard Jake groan and the other Cobras winger made a token effort to stop him. The Cobras defenders had both played it safe and were already back near the red line.

With nothing but open ice before him, Charlie

remembered his linemates still on the bench. Instead of continuing the attack he curled at his own blue line and took it back to the Sharks' end, passing to a defenceman behind the net. The Cobras players ignored him and hurried to change lines, although he noticed one of them gave him an odd look. He didn't care. At least it gave Simon and Gabriel the chance to get on.

Gabriel swung across the top of the circle and took a well-timed pass from the defenceman without breaking stride. Charlie swerved behind him and Gabriel dropped the puck back. Charlie took two steps with it and sent it cross ice to Simon, who in turn one-timed it to Gabriel breaking in. The quick passing took the Cobras forwards by surprise. Out of position, they could only look on as a three-on-two developed.

About four feet from the blue line, Gabriel left the puck and drove to his left. At the same time, Simon cut across to pick it up. Charlie sensed the defenders' confusion and drifted to the middle. Simon saw it too and left the puck again. The right defenceman foolishly lunged for it, only to have Charlie snatch it first. Now it was a three-on-one.

The play was over in seconds. The puck went from Charlie to Simon, back to Gabriel, and again to Charlie. The lone defenceman dropped to his knees, believing Charlie would shoot. Instead Charlie backhanded it to Gabriel, who drove to the near post forcing the goalie to drop to his butterfly. Charlie put on the breaks to give Gabriel a passing angle, while Simon set up at the far post.

Gabriel passed it across the crease to Simon. Unlike Corey, he showed patience. The goalie flung himself to that post, only to have Simon calmly flick it to Charlie, who guided it to Gabriel. Almost laughing, Gabriel one-timed it into the wide-open net.

Charlie looked at his linemates in disbelief. You could play an entire season and not see a goal like that. They'd gone the length of the ice to score. A miracle goal he'd never forget. All the frustration of this game, of the camp, simply disappeared. This was hockey magic, and from Simon and Gabriel's reaction he knew they felt the same.

Corey had jumped on the ice.

"Don't even think about it," Simon yelled. "We can handle the last thirty seconds."

"But you scored," Corey whined.

"That's the point," Gabriel shot back.

Binns had a foot on the boards. "Corey, for the last time, change when I tell you." Corey hung his head and returned to the bench.

"Nice goal to watch," Savard said, when they lined up for the draw.

Charlie grinned and put his stick down. Not a nice goal — the perfect goal, and the perfect way to end this camp. Charlie won the draw and a Sharks defenceman chopped it off the boards where Simon was able to dump it in. Burnett won the race to the puck and wired it around the wall. His winger knifed the puck to Savard and he broke over the blue line and lifted a soft back-hand down the ice. A Sharks defenceman corralled the spinning puck, but time had run out. He blasted a long shot from his own blue line, easily gloved by the goalie. The buzzer sounded and he flipped the puck high in the air. The Cobras descended on their goalie to congratulate him on the win.

Gabriel come up to Charlie from behind and slapped his shin pads. "They can't take that last one from us," he said.

Charlie slapped his shin pads back.

He was absolutely right.

STANDING "O"

The three linemates picked up their equipment and walked down the hall.

"We needed one more shift to tie it up," Gabriel said.

"We needed two more to win it," Simon said.

"And of course, one more shift for the insurance marker," Charlie said, and they all laughed.

"Amazing how quick this camp goes by. Feels like we just got here, and we're leaving in a few hours," Gabriel said seriously.

"It's been a long season, I tell ya," Simon said. "My team had a mini-camp at the end of August, and if you count tryouts in April, and then we had a tournament in May, it feels like I played all year. I get a break this summer for six weeks or so, and I'm right back at it."

"What are you doing this summer?" Charlie asked.

He grinned. "Going to hockey camp."

"Gotta play the game," Gabriel laughed. "I'm doing a one-week skills camp too."

Charlie understood, because he was cut from the same cloth. The game made up for it all — even when you didn't feel like hauling yourself out of bed for a seven a.m. practice.

He dropped his equipment to the ground when they got outside and held out his fist. "Let's keep in touch and tell me how your teams shape up once the season starts up again. Maybe we'll run into each other at a tournament or something."

"You'd better hope not," Simon said. "I know all your moves."

"I've kept my best ones back," charlie said. Gabriel and Simon punched his fist and they said goodbye. He picked up his bag and began walking to the dorm. Scott, Nick and Slogger were standing together in the field.

"You boys represented with pride," Charlie said to Nick and Slogger.

"Thanks, dude," Slogger said. "I liked that last goal."

"Excuse me, Slogger. I think Charles was talking to me," Scott said. "Yes, I did cheer well. Got a bit tired by the end of the second period and had to dig deep, but I felt I brought it big time in the third."

"The pom-poms were a nice touch," Nick said.

"And so was the skirt," Slogger added.

"I dominated — what can I say," Scott said.

They talked about the game as they made their way back. The buses were parked outside the dorm. The sight of them made Charlie a bit sad. Now that it was over, he didn't want to go. Jen was waiting for them by the doors.

"We have a tight schedule to keep, gentlemen," she began.

"As opposed to the loose schedule we usually keep," Scott said.

"You forgot about the twelve seconds she gave us to relax yesterday," Nick said.

Scott slapped his forehead. "I'm such a forgetter."

Jen laughed. "We're leaving in about two hours," she said. "Pack up and leave your bags by the buses. Coach Clark is going to address the players in Rink 1 before you depart. This is the last time you'll hear this from me — don't be late."

"You guys go ahead," Charlie said. "I just want to check out the University Store for a sec."

"Get me something nice," Scott cried, as he ran off.

* * *

Charlie zipped his bag closed and placed it on the floor. Corey had done the same, and their eyes met momentarily. Corey turned away first.

"Good game," Charlie said cautiously.

"It felt too short," Corey said. "I barely worked up a sweat. We were beginning to take over in the third. I figured out their goalie. You have to fake low and take it upstairs. My fault. I should've done that earlier. Could've bagged a couple of quick ones to keep us in it."

Charlie spotted his sweatshirt under his bed and reopened his bag.

"Did you see all the scouts watching the game? I bet there were at least seven of them," Corey said.

Charlie stuffed his sweatshirt in and zipped his bag shut.

"Just for the record," Corey continued, "I'm glad you got to play, and you had a good game. I'm not sure you did the right thing. I get the fact you wanted to protect Jake because he's from your hometown. The guy stole the ring, though. I don't think he should've been allowed to play."

That was going too far. "You've got to be joking, Corey. You and I know who . . ."

A knock stopped him. Before he could say anything the door flung open. A man walked into the middle of the room. Well-dressed, with a fancy brown leather jacket and highly polished shoes, he looked around the room, grimacing when he noticed Charlie. Corey flushed and lowered his eyes.

"Dad, this is Charlie . . . He was my roommate," Corey said softly.

Charlie said, "Hello," but he had to force himself not to laugh out loud. Corey's dad was tiny, shorter than Charlie. He looked more like the son than the father.

Mr. Sanderson glared back. "Um . . . hi . . . Charlie." He looked back at his son. "Quite a game this morning."

Corey sat on his bed. "I was just telling Charlie that it felt way too short and we were coming back. I just got going and the buzzer went."

"You call that going?" he said harshly. "Two shots on net all game, and you were on the ice for three of their goals. I thought Savard outplayed you, and that Wilkenson kid gave you all you could handle." He paused and looked closer at his son. "Didn't that Wilkenson get kicked out?"

"The coaches let him stay," Corey explained.

His dad waved him off. "Doesn't matter. Not a great way to end it; and not a great game to watch, at least from where I was sitting."

"I can do way better," Corey said weakly. "I was hurt at the beginning of camp — ask Charlie — and then I got sick, and maybe I'm still getting back . . ."

His dad shrugged. "Okay. Maybe. I know you were sick. Still . . ."

Charlie was taken aback. Corey was obviously unhappy about the way he played. His dad certainly wasn't making him feel any better.

"There were at least five Major Junior scouts in the stands, and another five college scouts. Do you think they were impressed? Does Corey Sanderson look like a prospect? Are they going to use a draft pick on you, or offer a scholarship?"

Corey was slumped over.

"I found it hard to get used to the lines," Charlie offered, trying to stall long enough to give Corey a chance to control himself in front of his dad. "Corey was just telling me that he only got going in the third period. I was sort of the same."

His dad stared at him until Charlie began to feel uncomfortable. Finally, he broke away and looked over at Corey. "Get your stuff packed and meet me downstairs in five minutes. I have back-to-back meetings at the office after we get home."

He whirled around and left. Corey didn't move. He sat on his bed, lost in thought. Charlie let him be, no longer wanting to confront him about the ring — or anything else. He felt so sorry for Corey that the other stuff didn't seem to matter.

Charlie had trouble thinking about his dad without getting sad or angry, but after seeing how Corey's dad treated him, the memory of his father was a little less painful. He put more pressure on himself than his father ever had. His dad had always been encouraging, teaching him stuff, taking care of him. He'd told him to play hockey because he loved the game. Maybe that was why hockey had become so important. He couldn't imagine life with a dad like Corey's.

Corey suddenly jumped to his feet, a determined look on his face. "Dad's totally right. I stunk the rink out. Shouldn't make excuses. That's for losers. I've been making too many excuses. I gotta work harder — put more effort into my training. I slacked off too much. You can do anything if you put your mind to it. That's what dad says; and he's right. Look at him. He built his business from scratch — all by himself. You gotta want it more than the other guy.

"This is my wake-up call. I gotta keep working on my game, and the next time I run into Savard or Wilkenson it'll be different. I promise you."

Charlie felt even worse than before. The poor guy would keep training himself to death in the hope that he'd get drafted or get a scholarship. Corey was wasting his life trying to impress his dad.

"You sure that's what you want to do? I mean, is it worth it?"

Corey suddenly looked desperate. "What else am I gonna do?" He shook his head several times. "That's not what I meant to say. The point is, you'll never make it with that attitude."

"Make what?"

"Make Junior . . . college . . . the NHL . . . Make it!" Corey's eyes blazed. He snatched his phone from the side table and stuffed it in his pocket. "Forget it. Not your worry. Gotta go." He picked up his bag. "Goodbye," he said.

Charlie didn't want things to end like this. "Hey, Corey. I didn't mean anything by it. I know you'll make it. And you did get hurt . . . and sick. Your dad didn't really see that. You've got what it takes. No question."

Corey lowered his bag slowly to the floor. "Thanks, Charlie. I appreciate that. Nice meeting you. Too bad we didn't get a chance to play together more." He grinned. "Maybe we'll play together in the NHL."

Charlie couldn't stay mad at him. "That would be awesome, Corey."

Corey slapped Charlie on the back and closed the door behind him. Seconds later, Slogger, Nick and Scott barged in. Charlie picked up his bag.

"Are you guys ready to go? Jen told us to hustle," Charlie said.

"Ladies and gentlemen," Nick announced. "I never thought I'd live to see the day when Charlie Joyce of Terrence Falls would tell us to hurry up so we wouldn't be late."

"Way to nail the concept of time when camp is over," Scott wisecracked.

"Maybe he wants to impress his new girlfriend," Nick offered.

"Julia will be jealous," Scott said.

"Who's Julia?" Slogger asked.

"Charlie's lady friend," Scott said. "Shocking how quickly he forgot her."

Charlie and Julia had become friends over the course of grade nine. Nick and Scott were forever teasing him about her.

"You guys are relentless," Charlie said.

Nick put his arm around his shoulders. "That's our job. We gotta keep you humble."

"You're good at it," Charlie quipped.

As they walked to the rink, Charlie told them about Corey's dad.

"I kinda thought he'd fess up," Charlie said. "Obviously, I know the truth."

"Probably too afraid to admit that he can't live up to his dad's expectations," Nick said.

"Problem is that Corey's maxed out as a player," Charlie said. "I don't think he's got a real shot. He should throttle it back and play for fun."

"Not likely." Scott punched his arm. "Not many people are as smart as us."

Most of the other players were already seated when they arrived.

Jen was at the top of the stairs. "Mr. Joyce, you're nothing if not consistent. And I see you've made your friends late for the last meeting as well."

"How can we be late?" Charlie said, exasperated with himself. "I thought we had lots of time."

Jen laughed. "I'm kidding, Charlie. I can't help giving you a hard time. You're so serious."

Charlie blushed. "Sorry. I guess I am."

She laughed again. "No need to apologize." She leaned closer. "You're a great kid. I admire what you did — all the staff does — and you had a great game today."

He felt himself blushing more. "Thanks . . . I just did what I thought was right."

"Not everyone does," she said, giving his arm a squeeze. "Now take a seat before you really are late."

"Julia's gonna be absolutely furious," Scott said.

"Joyce — the ladies' man," Nick added.

He tried to ignore them as they continued to kid him. Fortunately, Coach Clark and the rest of the coaching staff came in.

"It's been an unusual year, I'll give you that," Clark stated, and laughter filled the cavernous arena. "It's also been a very productive one. You all got a taste of a real hockey camp. I saw some hard work, and a great deal of skill development. Remember what you learned, keep practising and getting stronger, and I'm confident there are some future stars in this room."

He took a sip from his coffee mug. "When we first

started this camp we used to give out awards. Remember, Rick?"

Binns nodded.

"Then we decided we weren't sending the right message. This camp isn't about awards. It's about working hard for yourself, doing your best, and — I'm going to say it — having fun." A good-natured groan came from the players. "Too many kids are being treated like professional athletes already these days. Play because you want to, not because of big bucks in the NHL. There's nothing wrong with trying to make it as a pro — but many players are called and very, very, very few are chosen. School must be your first priority, along with family and friends.

"I'm proud of you all. Great work, and I hope to see some of you again."

He began clapping, and the rest of the coaching staff did too. The players joined in, and soon they were clapping in rhythm, as one cohesive unit — a team.

"I didn't expect him to say that," Charlie said in Slogger's ear.

"I think at least one person needed to hear it," Slogger said.

"I don't think we do," Charlie said.

He could take pride in that, and in how he hadn't quit when the going got tough. Things had looked bad for a while — really bad. But like Coach Clark had said, hockey is about working hard and doing your best. He'd done that, and ended up learning more than he ever imagined. Best of all he'd met some of the best, and coolest, guys around — Slogger, Simon and Gabriel to name a few. Sure, you had to put up with the likes of Jake and Zane. But even they couldn't ruin this experience.

This really was shaping up to be the best summer of his life.

He rose with the rest of the players as they continued to applaud.

BACK ON TRACK

His mom and grandparents greeted him at the door.

"You're going to have to hose him off," his grandma said. "Didn't they let you take showers at this camp?"

He kissed his grandparents. "Sorry, Grandma. I didn't have a lot of time to do laundry."

"I'm not that fussy," his mom said. "Give me a hug."

She put her arms around his neck and kissed him on the cheeks. "I missed my little boy."

"Not so little," his grandpa said. "I think you grew a few inches in the two weeks you were gone."

"Did you get enough to eat?" his grandma asked.

"We didn't starve."

"I bet you could use a snack," his mom said.

He grinned. "Maybe a little something."

"Come into the kitchen and tell us all about the camp," she said.

"Where's Danielle?" he asked.

"My goodness," his mom said. "Home less than a minute and you want to see your sister."

"I kinda got her a present and wanted to give it to her."

"She's in the back playing soccer with Hannah. Go say hi and tell them to come in for a snack too."

He grabbed a bag from his knapsack and hurried to the backyard. Danielle was playing goalie, while Hannah, her best friend, fired away.

"Take it easy on her," he called from the deck. "Goalie can't stop nothin'."

"Hey, Charlie's back!" Danielle squealed.

The two girls came running over.

"So what's in the bag?" Danielle asked, a big smile on her face.

Charlie laughed. "Not even a hello high-five?"

They each raised a hand and he slapped them both in one motion.

"Okay, so what's in the bag?" Danielle giggled.

"A few things," he announced. "I figured Hannah would be here, so I doubled up on these."

He pulled out two enormous lollipops.

Hannah gasped. "Thanks, Charlie. They're like the size of my head."

In no time the girls had the wrappers off.

"Didn't you say you had a few things in the bag?" Danielle said.

"I did. Danielle, close your eyes."

She covered her eyes with both hands.

"Follow instructions," he said good-naturedly. "I

can see you peeking between your fingers. Now, hold out your hands."

His mom and grandparents had come out on the deck. He gave her the bag.

"Wow, cool!" Danielle exclaimed. "Look, mom, a Northern University hockey sweater! It's like the real thing . . . NHL quality. I love it!"

"Put it on, Danny," he said.

"Very cool, D," Hannah said.

Everyone looked at her.

"You can all stop staring at me like I got chocolate sauce all over my face."

That got a good laugh.

"Why don't you three come in?" his mom said. "I've got some muffins and croissants."

"Yum!" Danielle shrieked, racing inside with Hannah trailing closely behind.

"That was very nice of you," his mom said as they were on their way back into the house. "Those jerseys cost a lot."

"I saved up some money from working this year at the café, and thought she'd like it."

"Weren't you saving up for a new long board?" his grandpa asked.

"A little bit . . . no big deal. I've got the rest of the summer to make it back. And Danielle deserved something special for giving up her drama camp."

"Come on," his mom said. "Let's join the girls before they finish everything off."

Charlie agreed gratefully, and was soon telling them

all about the camp, careful to leave out the problems Corey had caused. He did tell them about Corey's dad, however.

"So many parents live through their children," his mom said, "and put so much pressure on them that their kids quit playing."

"It's worse than that for Corey," Charlie said. "He's too afraid of his dad to ever stop. His dad's gonna freak if Corey doesn't get drafted into Junior or get a scholarship, and I really don't think he's good enough."

The phone rang and Danielle leapt up to get it. She handed it to him.

"It's a girl — Julia."

Charlie felt himself go beet red. "Hello?" he said tentatively.

It was Pudge. Danielle's mouth was full, and she was laughing so hard bits of croissant were spilling out. "I'll get you for that, little sister," Charlie joked. He spoke quickly to Pudge and hung up.

"Two questions, Mom. First question is: Can I go to Pudge's cottage next week? I had to cancel on him because of the camp and . . ."

"No problem, Charlie. That would be fun."

"And . . . the second question is . . ." He took a deep breath. "Is it okay if I go to The Hill with Pudge and maybe Scott, Nick and Zachary?"

His mom leaned back in her chair. "You've been home for what — an hour? — and . . ."

"I know, Mom. Sorry. It's just that everyone's going off to summer camps or cottages and stuff. This is like the last time we'll hang out all together until school."

His mom raised both eyebrows.

"We're gonna go out and play," Danielle said, as she stuffed more croissant into her mouth. She and Hannah charged out the back door.

His mom sighed. "I guess we've had enough family time."

His grandparents started to laugh. "Welcome to the teen years," his grandma said.

"So, is it okay?" Charlie asked.

"Of course. Dinner's at six."

"I'll be back."

"If it's on time, that'll be a first," his mom said.

"One thing I learned at hockey camp is the importance of punctuality. No more being late for this kid."

He hurried up the stairs to get his gear and headed out the door.

* * *

His friends were already at the top of The Hill when he arrived.

"Sorry guys. Had the grandparents over and stuff."

"Just got here myself," Nick said. "Parents weren't keen on me taking off either."

"You guys should try my method," Scott said. "I throw a tantrum until my parents are so ashamed they beg me to go."

"Dude, you are downright scary sometimes," Nick said.

"It's starting to concern me too," Scott said.

Charlie spotted a familiar figure approaching.

"Yo! Pudge. What's up?" Charlie said. They high-fived.

"How was camp?" Pudge said a bit shyly.

"Would it be too bogus for me to say it was over-the-top awesome?"

"It would make me a bit jealous, but I can deal."

Nick and Scott came over.

"Is Charlie telling you about how I totally out-skilled everyone at camp, and the coaches told me I was the best player they'd ever seen?" Scott said.

"He hasn't had time to fill me in on everything — but I'm sure he will . . . eventually."

"Who's ready to ride?" Zachary said, pulling up beside them.

"I'm game," Charlie said.

Zachary looked down at his board. "I thought you said you'd raised the cash for new wheels?"

"Not quite there yet. I'll have it in a month or two."

"Let's do a train," Zachary said. "Charlie, you're in behind me and hold on tight. The rest of you grab on."

"That seems a perfectly appropriate way to kill ourselves. Black Beauty and me are in," Scott said, patting his board.

"We're with ya," Nick and Pudge chorused.

Zachary rolled off, popped an ollie and did a nose grind to stop.

"You're right, Scott. We've lived long enough," Charlie said, grabbing hold of the back of Zachary's shirt.

Charlie heard voices coming towards them. He

recognized one — Jake's. As if he hadn't had enough of that guy.

Jake stopped talking when he spotted them.

"You guys go ahead. We're in no hurry," Jake said.

Charlie was confused — no insult, no challenge, no sarcasm? But he wasn't about to stick around and question it.

"Let's do this," he said, pushing Zachary forward.

Pudge grabbed his shirt, and Nick and Scott followed. They moved slowly at first, snaking down the hill to build momentum, until the first corner when they really got going.

Charlie crouched lower on his board and leaned into the turn, the wind whipping through his hair.

"Not fast enough, boys! Time to fly!" he shouted.

ABOUT THE AUTHOR

David Skuy spent most of his childhood playing one sport or another — hockey, soccer, football, rugby. Now he is a writer and lawyer who lives in Toronto, Ontario with his wife and two kids. He still plays hockey once a week and remains a die-hard Leafs fan.

He began writing the Game Time series to try to capture the competition, the challenges, the friendships and the rivalries that make sports so much fun.

The Game Time series:

Off the Crossbar
Rebel Power Play
Making the Cut